JULIA

JULIA

JOHN LUCAS

GREENWICH EXCHANGE
LONDON

Greenwich Exchange, London

First published in Great Britain in 2019
All rights reserved

John Lucas © 2019

Printed and bound by imprintdigital.com
Cover design: December Publications
Tel: 07951511275

Greenwich Exchange Website: www.greenex.co.uk

Cataloguing in Publication Data
is available from the British Library

Cover Art reproduced courtesy of Shutterstock

ISBN: 978-1-910996-27-0

in memory of Ross Martin

I

1

LIGHT GLITTERED ON WATER, SHARP AS knives.

From under the canvas shade of the beach's taverna, Julia felt free to gaze across the sand to where a man, hugely fat, sprawled by the water's edge, three small children scampering between him and a woman, almost as fat as he was, decked out in a flowered bikini, who lay on her side, head propped on hand. She laughed in encouragement as she watched the children trickle sand onto the man's bare torso then rub it over the vast swelling of his stomach. Without opening his eyes, the man grabbed the smallest child by one hand and swung it aloft. It screamed in joyous terror as it dangled in its father's secure grip and the other two children began to scream in unison as they darted in and out of reach. Finally one jumped onto his free hand and the man, yelling in pain, sat clumsily up and deposited the child he had been holding onto the sand beside him, and, while he rubbed his injured hand, shouted angrily at the pair as they ran to their mother, herself now in a sitting position, and cowered behind her.

'How very unlike the home lives of our own dear families.'

Julia turned to look at the speaker, who was sitting at the opposite end of the table. Giles Poynter was in profile, his still-black hair, prominent nose and deep jaw line above a bare torso, tanned by Greek sun.

The others ignored his remark. They were busy helping Tassos spread a paper cover across the two tables he had dragged together before he could unload from a large wooden tray the plates of food they had ordered. Fried zucchini balls, grilled sardines, sliced and

11

grilled aubergine, small triangular cheese pies, fried calamari, bowls of salad.

Behind Tassos a young boy waited patiently, gripping in both hands a tray on which were six glass tumblers, the same number of wine glasses, and, laid on their sides, two plastic bottles of water.

'And now I go for your wine,' Tassos said, watching approvingly as his son arranged the glasses before gripping the cap of one of the bottles, finally managing to unscrew it and place it on the table.

'Beer for me,' Julia's husband said.

'Me too. It's too hot for wine.'

'It's *never* too hot for retsina.' Giles's mocking rebuke was directed at the young man sitting beside him. 'Besides, when in Greece ... '

He smiled across at Julia, wanting her agreement.

'I'll drink water,' she said.

He shrugged, indifferent.

'Two for beer, three for wine – I think that calls for a full carafe – and for Julia – well now, what shall it be? Still or sparkling? Any particular vintage?' Making no answer to his question, trying to ignore the amused disdain in his look, she reached for the opened water bottle, poured herself a tumbler-full, drank it down in two gulps, and re-filled her glass. But when she made to return the cap the bottle slipped from her grasp and spilled some of its contents on the table.

'Plastered on plastic,' the man murmured. 'Whatever next.' He looked round the table, inviting their answering smiles.

'Oh, for god's sake.'

The young man, having muttered the words to himself, was staring down at his plate. His nose and jaw line made plain his kinship with the man who sat at the head of the table and Julia would have known him to be Giles Poynter's son even if Giles hadn't taken pains to remind them all who he was when the two of them appeared half an hour ago. Giles was the last to arrive for the beach lunch that had been planned – as such lunches were always planned – to celebrate or, as some said, mourn what its regular attenders knew as 'exodus'. They would all be leaving the island within the next few days. Back to England, ready, most of them, to confront what Giles, with a smirk, called the coal face of academic life, summer at an end, the strained joviality of beach and taverna meetings locked away for another year.

Julia and Martin had shared a taxi with James and his new partner from the port town where they were staying in adjacent hotels. By tacit agreement they were to arrive at the beach before Giles, who over the years had come to take for granted the right of being last to arrive, and, having been greeted by Tassos, the quartet commandeered a table for them all and sat to await his coming.

Soon enough the beach buggy Giles always hired for his month on the island came bouncing and slewing down the stony, dust-matted track that led to the beach, and they watched as he and his son, newly arrived on the island, clambered out and waded through sand towards their table.

Giles stood slightly behind the young man as he announced, 'For those who may not recall, this is Orlando, no longer an adolescent whipper-snapper as when you saw him last, but a man of the world, newly degreed. And should you, Orlo, have forgotten, let me re-introduce my old friends Julia and Martin Gibbs and James Piper and his ... his partner.' For a moment he made a show of letting his poise falter before he stepped to the young man's side, saying as he did so, 'Orlando has come down from his seaside university, where he will return to launch himself into society at large.'

'Not *down*,' the young man said. 'I've finished with the place. That's all.'

'That's not what you told me last night.' Giles looked around the table. 'I am privy to the information that Orlando and a group of graduate friends are planning to found a community newspaper in the town where they passed their undergraduate years and which they have come to know well. Probably too well. Dens of vice, caverns of iniquity, haunts of shame. That sort of thing. And as a result of their experiences, they intend to alter the possibilities of journalism as we know it. Them.'

Giles made to put an arm round his son, but the young man shrugged him off.

Giles raised his hands in mock supplication. 'Youth today,' he said.

He glanced towards the seats that had been left empty, took the one which immediately became head of table and motioned his son to the other beside James, who, as he indicated the woman sitting opposite him, said to the two newcomers,'Let me introduce Trudy.'

'Welcome aboard,' Giles said.

His son said nothing.

James's partner, looking from one to the other, said, 'You'll have to forgive me. I'm new to all this.' Her voice was neutral and, after a brief glance around the table, returned to studying her ringless hands as they lay clasped beside her plate.

Unlike the others, who were all in casual shirts and jeans, she was wearing a white sleeveless dress. Dark, wavy hair was carefully styled and allowed a glimpse of pearl earrings. For all her reserve she seemed at ease, and, as she raised her eyes to meet Julia's, as though suspecting she was being looked at, Julia saw the glimmer of a smile on her lips. Then it was gone.

Passing Trudy a plate of the cheese pies, Giles said, 'New today, gone tomorrow.' But seeing her look of puzzlement he had the grace to add, 'You're new to us, I mean, and we'll be gone tomorrow. Sadly.'

His son stood abruptly up. 'I'm going for a walk,' he said, and when his father called after him, 'What about food?' he shouted back without turning his head, 'Not hungry.'

Julia watched him make his way across sand to the track down which he and his father had recently driven.

'Sorry about that,' Giles said. 'The more observant among you will have noticed that not all is as well as could be hoped for with my beloved son. His nerves are frayed by overnight travel, and, I suspect, an unsuccessful love affair.' The words, spoken lightly enough, masked, Julia sensed, a deeper irritation, discomposure even. Giles, as she – as they all – had learned over the ten or so years they had been coming to the island, took care to present to them an unrufflable front. A man of assured charm, of unassertive but implied control, that was Giles, or how Giles at least liked to present himself and, according to Martin, it was how he had appeared from the day he, Martin and James first met as university students. It came to her, then, that until this day she had never thought of Giles as a family man. True, in the early years of these annual holidays, Giles and Tessa had brought the young Orlando and his brother Corin with them, much as Martin and she had been accompanied by Polly. But of late, the parents had been on their own, and mention of children was at best brief and to the point. James, after all, with his succession of girlfriends, had no interest in families. Besides, Giles and Tessa always seemed sufficient unto themselves.

She made herself listen to Martin's emollient words. 'I can't think when we last saw Orlando. Six or seven years ago, at a guess. We must seem a bit long in the tooth to him.'

'Speak for yourself,' James said. He had taken off his sweat shirt and now sat, a thick matting of hair almost covering his torso. He grinned across at Trudy whose answering smile was accompanied by a raised eyebrow.

'Me Tarzan,' Julia said.

* * *

Early that evening, some hours after the beach party had broken up with a final toast to enduring friendship, Julia and Martin sat under a tree in the garden of their waterfront hotel. Above them, a noisy congregation of sparrows all but drowned out the cicadas' persistent ratcheting, and Julia had to speak more loudly than she wished.'Tomorrow's our last day, and I am *not* prepared to spend it in the company of that man.'

Martin sat silent. Then, sighing, he said, 'I thought we agreed to meet for a lunchtime drink.'

'I agreed to nothing,' Julia said. 'You can do as you like, but I've had quite enough of Giles for one year.' Or for ever, she almost added.

'He's not that bad.'

'Let's just say that I'm beginning to feel I'd rather chew broken glass than be in his presence.'

'What will you do, then?'

'Please myself. Walk around town, peer in at shops. Oh, and I need to get something for Polly. Her birthday's coming up, don't forget.'

'I hadn't,' Martin said. 'Polly's twenty-fifth. It makes a man feel very old.' He sighed dramatically. 'Our little girl, twenty-five. It doesn't seem possible. And to think, Mother, how she used to spend the summers with us in our island retreat.'

'Until she grew up and found more enjoyable ways of spending her free time. As did Orlando. God, wasn't that embarrassing, the way Giles spoke about him? No wonder he was so keen to take himself off. And Corin of course never comes.'

'Too busy. Corin's got his own rock group,' Martin said in his usual voice, 'Much in demand, by all accounts.'

'You mean by Giles's account. "My son, the *rock* musician."' And Julia made a fair imitation of the ersatz shudder of disapproval which accompanied Giles's words.

'Not only his.' Martin reached for the glass of gin and tonic on the small stone table beside him. 'Corin – or Nic as he calls himself – is a big draw. Queues round the block for black-market price tickets wherever he plays. One of my research students told me. She's a big fan. When I mentioned that I knew him, and after she'd picked herself up, she begged me to use "my influence" to get her a ticket.'

'You never told me that.'

'Didn't I? Well, there was nothing to tell. I had to confess that it was his parents I was friendly with and that I hadn't seen Nic himself since he was Corin the teenager. My influence was therefore minimal.' Then, changing the subject, he asked, 'Did Tessa say anything to you about why she was going back early?'

'No. But we can guess, can't we? The usual problem, or so I imagine.' She paused. 'I'm surprised that Orlando came, weren't you? Not that it took him long to realise he could do without his father's charmed circle. *Orlando.* What a name.' She lay back in her chair and stared up at the shaking branches where invisible sparrows bickered and an occasional leaf floated down, one settling on her arm. 'Not his fault, I know,' she said, brushing the leaf away, ' but quite enough to make him want to sever any connection with whoever wished the name on him, poor lad. Which I'm willing to bet was Giles.'

For a few minutes they sat in silence. It was broken by a sudden splutter of laughter from Julia.

'What's so funny?' Martin asked, drowsily.

'I was thinking of your defence of Master Giles as "Not bad". He'd love you if he heard that was how you thought of him. Giles, commander of men. *Not bad.*' A further pause, after which she turned to her husband. 'You're not so bad yourself,' she said, leaning over to stroke the arm nearer her.

Martin turned his face to hers and they exchanged smiles, wary, affectionate. She reached to run her hand over his stubbly brown hair, now flecked with grey, and he caught her fingers, kissed them one by one. 'I love you,' he said.

'And I love you.' She freed her hand, wriggled upright in her chair. 'But I am not, repeat *not*, going to spend my last day on the island in Giles's presence. Is that understood?'

'Understood,' Martin said.

2

THE FOLLOWING MORNING THEY LINGERED OVER breakfast, taken as always on the hotel terrace. From there, they gazed out at the sea, from time to time turning to smile silently at each other, neither wanting to speak the words both knew the other was thinking.

But they were spoken by Andreas as he came to clear away their plates. 'Your last full day, my dear friends. Tomorrow you will be once more in England.'

'Afraid so,' Martin said.

'But it is not so bad,' the hotel owner said. 'Next year you will come again to my hotel. And I will have your room ready for you. Is it not so?' And he smiled his sleepy lidded smile. 'You take the early morning ferry, I think? I shall of course order you a taxi.'

'And I shall come to settle our bill,' Martin said.

'Of course,' Andreas said, 'but please, do not hurry.'

He turned, bearing the tray on which were their used breakfast things, and padded away.

This time the smile Martin and Julia exchanged was one of wry acknowledgement. As always, Andreas had made his point. They must pay him today because there was no chance that tomorrow he would be up in time to wave them goodbye. Andreas was a night bird. Each evening he made a slow progress round the waterfront bars, seldom returning to his hotel before the early hours. His daughter, Maria, by now nearer to thirty than twenty, but still, despite the attentions of various young men, unmarried and likely to remain so while her father safeguarded her honour and thereby his hotel's arrangements, was on morning duty. But although entrusted with breakfasts and early departures and arrivals she was not allowed to have any part in financial matters.When Andreas referred to 'my hotel' he meant what he said.

***

An hour later, by which time Julia had packed and Martin had paid, it was time for them to go their separate ways. Martin, in maroon sports shirt and jeans that set off his still slender frame, kissed his wife firmly on the lips before he went to join the other two men for what would no doubt be a long, boozy lunch at Pavlos's waterfront bar, leaving Julia, also in jeans and wearing a green top, free to wander the little town's back streets, window-shopping and choosing gifts for Polly as well as for the few friends with whom the exchange of presents bought on what they called their 'travels' was an annual ritual.

About to enter a favourite shop, one that sold inexpensive but attractive items of jewellery as well as a variety of ceramics, she stood aside for a woman who was on her way out. It was Trudy. Well, well.

Trudy's smile was one of genuine warmth, and when she said 'Oh, hello', the words, plain in themselves, suggested a pleasure in meeting that deserved an equally welcoming response.

'Buying or merely looking?' Julia asked, adding, 'I like coming here. It's a happy hunting ground. Presents for all the family. Well, all women members, anyway.'

Trudy held up a small package, neatly wrapped and tied. 'A bracelet. For my mother,' she said. She was wearing a pale green calf-length dress, her bare arms set off by slim, dark-wood bangles, and with her hair tied back she looked entirely at her ease. Yesterday's reserve had vanished.

'Fancy a coffee?' Julia asked on impulse.

'I'd love a coffee.'

'In that case,' Julia said, 'I know the perfect place.'

A few minutes later the two of them were sitting at a café by the harbour, gazing out at the ranks of yachts, of small fishing craft, of dinghies, and beyond them and the harbour wall, some half-mile distant, a wooded islet seeming to shimmer in the still heat of noonday air, and, further off, and forming a continuous backdrop to the milkily opalescent sea, the mountainous outline of the Greek mainland.

'Isn't it ... isn't it beautiful?' Trudy said. She sighed.

'Your first time in Greece?' Julia asked the young woman, touched by the innocent candour of her words.

'Some years ago I came on a package holiday to Crete.'

'And?'

'It rained every day of the week.'

'Bad luck,' Julia said, moving her bag from the table they sat at to allow the waiter in his white, short-sleeved shirt and black trousers, to set between them their Americanos and two filled glasses of water.

'And how many more days are you staying?' She knew that James, who had arrived later than the others, would almost certainly have booked for a full month.

'We're here for another week.' As Trudy spoke she flapped her hand to disperse clouds of tobacco smoke that drifted across from the next table where a group of men of all ages clustered, all of them smoking, all of them talking at once, slamming their hands down on the table, occasionally bursting into laughter or, to the accompaniment of ritual gestures, shouting as if in anger.

'Do *all* Greeks smoke *all* of the time?' Trudy asked.

'Most of them,' Julia said, 'but only during waking hours and especially where there are signs asking them not to. Still, if you're here for another week you'll have time for swimming. Wash off the fumes.'

'I will, now that I know there's no tide to carry me off.' Trudy looked at her, her smile conspiratorial.

Julia laughed. 'Giles can be a pain in the bum, I know. Never off duty.' Putting on a deep voice, deeper than Giles's even, she said, 'I think I should point out that the Mediterranean is a tideless sea. Miss ... Miss.' Then, in her own voice, she asked, 'What *is* your surname, by the way?'

'Cosgrove,' Trudy said. 'That little lecture of his was like being back in class.'

'Oh, nothing Giles likes better than lecturing, especially if he thinks

20

he's got a newcomer in his sights. He could see you were a bit unsure. You were, weren't you?' And when Trudy nodded, Julia said, 'Well, not to be wondered at, especially with Giles strutting his stuff. "The Mediterranean is tideless, the Saronic Gulf is part of the Aegean which is part of the Mediterranean. It therefore follows that the water beside which we sit, forming as it does part of said Gulf, is tideless."'

'And all because that poor man got soaked when the wave drenched him.' But Trudy was smiling, relaxing into talk.

Julia laughed, remembering the shout, *malakas*, a mixture of alarm and outrage that had come from the mountainous Greek as he was soused by the onrush of water which, like a mini tsunami, heaved itself ashore, washing over his recumbent body before it receded, sucked back into the tideless gulf.

Trudy, joining in the laughter, said, 'But if that wasn't incoming tide, what *was* it?'

'No idea,' Julia said, 'but it happens at about that time every afternoon. Martin used to tell our daughter that it was Poseidon waking from his siesta.'

'Your daughter?'

'Polly,' Julia told her. 'When she was younger she came with us to the island. But, can you believe it, once she reached student years other delights lured her away? As they did Orlando. I'm not sure why he bothered to make a return visit. He seemed bored out of his mind.'

Trudy, finishing her coffee, said, 'You don't look old enough to have a student daughter.'

The men at the next table were now standing, arguing loudly about who was to pay the bill. The two women watched them throw money onto the table, wave to the waiter, who waved back, then, in twos and threes, they crossed the strip of road to the quayside, where they sat astride motorbikes, revving their engines as they shouted to each other words of farewell and then, finally, in a haze of blue, foul-smelling exhaust fumes, drove off astride their puttering, farting machines.

Waiting until the noise had dwindled away, Julia said, 'Polly isn't a student any longer. Her twenty-fifth birthday is coming up next week.'

She gave a small, involuntary shudder. 'Time's winged chariot,' she said.

'James says you've all been coming here for years.'

'Years and years,' Julia said, 'I think this is our eleventh anniversary. Did James tell you how it all started?'

Trudy sipped from her water glass. 'He told me that you were at university together. The Wild Bunch.' She was now altogether less tentative.

'Far from it. We were hard-working students, I'll have you know. Well, the four of us were. Giles, Martin, James and me.'

There was a pause while Trudy absorbed this information. Julia looked at their empty coffee cups. 'Would you like to join me in a glass of wine?' she asked. 'Or do you have other plans?'

'I'd love a glass of wine,' Trudy said. 'I thought I'd be on my own today. I assumed you'd be with the others.' Her smile mingled relief with pleasure.

Julia waved to the waiter and when he came she asked him in Greek for a half-carafe of local barrel retsina. 'But it almost certainly won't be retsina,' she told Trudy as he went to fetch the wine. 'The Greeks seem to have become convinced that nobody but themselves likes their own beautiful wine. More likely he'll bring us a poor white substitute.'

But to her delight, after she'd poured for them both and they'd raised and clinked glasses, she discovered that they had after all been given genuine retsina. 'Honeyed sunlight,' she said, having swallowed, 'that's what Martin calls it.'

'With just a splash of sea,' Trudy said, sipping.

Julia laughed. 'What connoisseurs we'd make,' she said. 'That salty taste is the resin. It keeps the wine from going bad. Now, where were we?'

'You were telling me about how you all came to spend summers on the island.'

'So I was,' Julia said. 'Right, to avoid boring the socks off you, I'll keep this short.' And, taking a deep breath, she rattled through the relevant details: how she and Martin had married soon after leaving university; how Giles had been Best Man – 'he insisted' – ; how, a year or so later, he,

Giles, had married one of his students at the university where he had his first lectureship; how James had been *his* Best Man; how they'd all kept in touch, though not seeing much of each other, and then how, ten years later, when Martin's first book had received a good deal of attention in the national press, he was invited to Athens by the British Council. 'At that time James was working as a language teacher in Athens, so he stayed with him, and James brought him across for a day's visit. Martin came back full of it, told me he'd fallen in love with the place, wanted to take me to see it, so that summer we came here and James came to visit us, bringing Giles and Tessa with him because they were staying with him in Athens. And we decided – well, the three men decided – we'd make the island our annual meeting place. Friends re-united. And,' she said by way of a conclusion, 'we've been coming here ever since, at first with our kids, but more recently without them. Here endeth the story.'

'Not quite,' Trudy said.

'Oh?' Julia re-filled their glasses. Across from where they sat she watched the approach to harbour of the local, one o'clock ferry, passengers from nearby islands crowding at the stern as a crew member made a series of operatic gestures to guide the steersman into the ferry's accustomed berth.

'Sorry,' she said, aware that she had missed Trudy's question.

'I was asking about Giles's marriage,' Trudy said. 'James hinted that it was under ... ' And she stopped, blushing faintly. 'Now I'm sorry,' she said, picking up her wine glass. 'I'm an outsider, I oughtn't to be so nosy.'

'I guess it's an open secret that Tessa has a good deal to put up with,' Julia told her. 'As well as being rather too fond of the sound of his own voice, Giles is a bit too fond of the ladies.'

'You don't like him?'

'I certainly don't like what power has done to him.'

'As in pulling power?'

'You could call it that,' Julia said, matching Trudy's questioning smile. All the young woman's former hesitancy had vanished. 'Now that he's become a Dean or whatever his university calls it, he seems to think – he certainly *acts* – as though he's entitled to whatever he thinks he wants.'

'He's a bit old for students, surely?'

'Oh, he wouldn't dare to get near a student. Not nowadays. Harassment, it would be called. He'd be out on his ear, and quite right, too. But there are plenty of other women he's free to lust after. Secretaries, for instance.'

'Like me,' Trudy said.

'He surely hasn't tried it on with you?' Julia began to say, then stopped. 'Oh, lord,' she said. 'That sounds rude. Let me guess. You mean you're James's secretary?'

'Correct. I *am* James's secretary.' Trudy emptied her glass, rolled the stem round in manicured fingers. 'But I like my work. I'm not an office girl.' Her smile suggested an amused reproof of what Julia might have been assuming. And, as though deciding she needed to say more, she added, 'I'm what's called a personal secretary, which means that I get to see the world. James takes me with him when we're doing deals with foreign TV stations. He needs my linguistic skills. I love it. I've flown with him to Paris, Rome, Stockholm ... Full bed and board.' Her smile this time left no doubt what she meant.

Julia was having to revise entirely yesterday's view of Trudy Cosgrove. The woman facing her across their small, zinc-topped table was, she realised, as candidly open as she was assured.

As though to confirm this, Trudy said, casually, 'After all, James isn't married. And I like him.'

Julia shared out the rest of their wine. 'So do I,' she said. 'He's very personable I know, and Martin and I have always found him easy to be with.'

'And,' Trudy said, dispelling the last hint of restraint, 'he's good in bed.' Picking up her glass, she laughed, showing off her white, flawless teeth. 'Which helps,' she said.

***

As they finished their packing that evening, Julia told Martin of her chance meeting with Trudy and their conversation. 'I don't think she has any illusions about James,' she said. 'She told me that she knew about his reputation as someone who liked to play the field, but that it doesn't bother her. I'd say that she's well able to look after herself.'

'And you believe her?' Martin, having locked his case, was sitting on the side of the bed, watching Julia fold into her overnight bag odds and ends that she might need before they arrived back at Heathrow.

'Yes, I do.' Julia straightened up from her task. 'She more or less told me that their relationship is easy-as-it-goes. She's very different from how she seemed on the beach.'

'Ah, well, she was meeting us for the first time yesterday. James may have given her the impression he'd be introducing her to the Brains Trust.' He paused for dramatic effect. 'Eggheads United. All lucubration and no laughs.'

'She was prepared to laugh at Giles's lecture on tideless seas. And what *is* lucubration?'

'Over-elaboration in speech or writing. And before you say "That's Giles" remember he was our Best Man.'

'As I told Trudy Cosgrove.'

'And did she tell you much about herself?'

'Not much, but we exchanged addresses, agreed to keep in touch. Though I probably won't ever see her again. By this time next year James will no doubt have another girl and Trudy will be gone from his life. No tears, no fuss, Hooray for us.'

'Let's hope so,' Martin said. 'But I've known some of James's affairs to end in tears, though rarely his own.'

Julia came to sit on the bed beside him, taking his hand as she did so. 'Ours won't, will it?'

He inclined his head to hers, kissed her on the nose. 'Till death do us part,' he said.

'Good,' she said, kissing him back. 'Now, tell me about your day.'

He groaned. 'Do I have to? It was a lot less fun than yours. I don't know how much more of Giles I can stand. Every damned conversation led back to his crucial role in providing a steady hand at the tiller to pilot his institution towards – oh, I can't remember, was it the high seas of pro-active vision or the forward planning needed in these troubled, not to say tempestuous, times?' He paused. 'He surely didn't talk like this in

25

earlier days, did he?' He looked at his wife in appalled, half-comic appeal.

'I always thought Giles was born under the star of pompous windbag,' Julia said. 'What saved him from fully-inflated prattishness was that you and James, both of you, shoved enough pins into him to puncture his self-regard.'

'Well, we can't manage it nowadays.' Martin's laugh was rueful. 'I was hoping that Orlando might show up and lighten the conversational load, but no such luck. I gather he's only here because his father agreed to pay his air fare. After all the hard work he'd put in so as to get his degree, Giles explained, "I thought he deserved a break." Now, you're meant to ask what class of degree Orlando got, and I'm meant to tell you that *of course* it was a First. Of course, of course. What else for Giles's son. And then, guess what?'

'Giles bought a round,' Julia said.

Martin shook his head. 'No such luck. No, he wanted to know when exactly I'd be off to San Francisco. He was angling for an invitation, wanted a chance to parade himself before big chiefs on the West Coast. He went so far as to say that he'd welcome the chance to compare notes with "academic brethren" in the States.'

'I hope you told him to drop dead.'

Martin laughed briefly. 'I told him that I'd only be gone a month and would be keeping my head down while I was there.'

'Trudy knew about your Fellowship,' Julia said. 'James had told her. She seemed surprised I'd not be going with you. "I'd make sure James took me," she said.'

'And?'

Julia stood up, went to look out of their window at the sun sliding down behind the far-off mountains. Speaking with her back to her husband, she said 'I explained that I had responsibilities here, I mean in England, and that I couldn't afford to take time off from my teaching duties.'

She turned back to him. 'The problem of being a part-timer. No privileges, no concessions, no time off unless you want to risk not getting your work back, and I don't.'

'I'd love you to come with me,' Martin said.

'I know and I'd love to be with you. But it *is* only a month,' Julia said, 'as I explained to Trudy. And there will be other opportunities. With your reputation,' she added. 'That's no doubt what eats at Giles's soul. He's jealous. Wishes *he* was known as a leading authority on ... on anything.'

'Being an authority on Byzantine History is hardly as important as being Dean of Arts and thus responsible for developing a valid vision for enhanced viability.'

Laughing, Julia came back and, as she sat down next to Martin, she said, 'if you ever speak to me of valid visions I swear I'll sue for divorce.' She giggled. 'Perhaps that's what Tessa's now doing.'

'No,' Martin said, 'Giles told us that Tessa left early because her mother's ill.'

Putting an arm round her husband and drawing him close to her, Julia said, 'Let's hope her mother's real name is Sid the Seducer.' She licked his ear. 'I'm thinking of calling you Sid,' she said.

After a moment or two, she asked, 'How do you like that?'

'Very much,' Martin said.

3

JULIA DROVE MARTIN TO THEIR LOCAL STATION. From there he could take a mid-afternoon train to St Pancras and be at Heathrow in good time for his overnight flight to San Francisco. 'I'll be there almost before I've left,' Martin had said when they'd talked through his coming adventure the previous evening, he not bothering to hide his excitement, she trying to tamp down her envy. They'd been apart before – Martin was much in demand on the international conference circuit – but rarely for more than a few days and then only when he accepted British Council invitations to give a mini-series of lectures at various cities, among them Strasbourg, Geneva, Bucharest, all of which they'd subsequently visited together.

America was different. 'I don't suppose I'll ever get to see the West Coast now,' Julia said as Martin poured the last of the red wine that had accompanied the meal over which she'd taken much care, the last meal they'd enjoy together for a month, she thought mournfully, and probably the last proper meal she'd bother to prepare before his return. Eating on your own wasn't, after all, much fun.

Looking at her over his glass, Martin said defensively, 'Well, love, it was your decision not to come.'

'That's unfair,' she said, trying not to sound irritable. 'You know perfectly well the decision wasn't mine to make. The College said no, and that was that.' She watched as Martin began to gather up their used plates. 'Part-timers always get the worst deal. If I'd been on a full-time contract I'd have got away with it.' She twisted her mouth in an ironic smile. 'At the worst I could have got a part-timer to stand in for me.'

Standing now, he bent to kiss the top of her head. 'At least you've had your month in the sun.'

'And you're about to have another.' But she managed to keep resentment out of her voice.

'It's probably wet where I'm going,' he said. 'Or foggy.'

'Hardly worth going in that case.' She surrendered her glass to him. 'You can get all the rain and fog you want in dear old England.'

'I'll try not to notice the weather,' he said, as he took their plates away.

As they kissed the following afternoon and she stood back to watch him wheel his case through the ticket barrier, she called out, 'Don't forget. I want to hear from you the minute you've arrived', and hearing the nervousness in her voice, he smiled reassuringly as, shouldering the black bag in which he carried his laptop, he called back, 'No worries, mate.'

Then he was gone.

* * *

'Guess what, I've seen my first Hippy. Embalmed, of course.' Martin's voice was muffled, less she guessed by distance than fatigue, when he phoned to report his safe arrival, a guess he confirmed when, having added that he was speaking from bed, he promised a fuller conversation later, 'once I've had a chance to sleep off this jet-lag.'

'Poor you.' But he ignored her irony. 'I'm missing you already,' he said,'Take care. I love you.'

'I love you too,' she said, though as she spoke the line went dead.

She replaced the receiver, then, almost immediately had to pick it up again. Polly's voice said, 'Mum, have you heard from Dad yet? He must be there by now?'

'He is and I have. I've only this minute put the phone down. Mission accomplished. Dad's fine, although he needs to sleep off the effects of his plane journey.'

'And how are you?'

'Me? I'm fine, though I'd feel even better if I were there, rather than here. Still, as your gran used to say, "Mustn't grumble."'

'That's good. Mum, can you cope on your own for a couple of weeks?'

Slightly piqued by the question and the condescension it seemed to imply, Julia said, 'Dad's gone for a month, and it won't be the first time I've been left to my own devices.'

But Polly cut across her words. 'Oh, I know you'll be alright. Sorry, it was my clumsy way of telling you that Al and I are off to France for a fortnight. Going tomorrow.'

'Just like that?'

'Just like that. Snap decision. We both have two weeks' holiday owing to us and we thought "Well, why not?" So we booked ferry tickets last night and we're off early in the morning, just as the sun is rising.' The last words were trilled.

'By car?'

'Of course. We want to explore, go wherever the mood takes us, no plans beyond the next auberge.'

Polly's voice was full of excitement, of joy, even. 'I'll phone you regularly, promise, make sure I keep you in touch with our whereabouts.' She let out a modified whoop. 'Two weeks away from the office, I can't tell you how much I need *that*.'

'Obviously,' Julia said, 'Well, enjoy yourselves, and give my love to Al.'

'I will,' Polly said, 'And he sends his love. And love to Dad. Tell him to send me a card. Have to rush, Mum, we're going out for a bite of supper, then an early night. Just think, by this time tomorrow we'll be sitting down to dinner somewhere in France.' She paused and said, 'You're *sure* you'll be alright?'

'Quite sure,' Julia said and put the phone down.

'Quite sure,' she repeated to herself as she prepared her own evening meal. As so often when Martin was away she couldn't be bothered to cook. A rummage through the fridge produced enough salad materials for her to fill a plate, and a slice of yesterday's bread, toasted and spread with cottage cheese, provided all she needed. That, and a glass from an open bottle of Sancerre.

After she had washed her plate and glass under running water, she filled the kettle. 'A cup of tea, a slice of cake, but no Thou singing beside me in the wilderness,' she said to herself, waiting for the water to boil. Not that Leicester could be described as a wilderness, but, stirring her tea-bag, she allowed herself a moment's self pity. Martin gone and now Polly.

On impulse she took her tea upstairs, stood in Polly's room as she drank it. My little girl, a grown woman with a lover. She ran her gaze over the wall posters of rock groups she'd barely heard of, peered in at the wardrobe, virtually empty apart from one or two items Polly couldn't bear to throw away, including a denim skirt and long purple velvet blouse she'd worn to teenage parties at the houses of various friends, most of whom had vanished or long been abandoned. Blown to the wind's four quarters. Photographs of some of them were jammed into the frame of the mirror propped above Polly's desk, mugging for the camera, faces alive with the expectancy of youth, one or two even with braces on their teeth. How young they were, how untried, how apparently fearless.

Was it a sentimental indulgence for her to keep the room untouched? Since her move to London, Polly rarely returned, life in the big city being so much more exciting. And now there was Al, like Polly working for an advertising agency which Al sardonically remarked sold lies at premium rates. He'd made the comment when Polly first brought him to meet her parents. Sitting at their dinner table, the young man took wry pleasure in explaining to his hosts the concept of 'value engineering,' as it was known in the trade. 'Take soup, for example. Company A starts up a business selling soup in cartons. Good stuff, going well in the supermarkets. Company B thinks "we want a piece of this action." But if it's going to sell into the chain stores it needs to market the soup more cheaply than Company A.'

'Why not make better soup?' Martin asked. '"Soup for the discriminating palate." Surely good advertising could promote that. *Top of the Range.* Put a picture on the side of the carton: a saucepan simmering on top of a stove. How about that?'

Polly laughed. 'Clever old Dad,' she said, her smile ironic, almost pitying. 'No chance. It wouldn't work.'

'Why not?' Julia wanted to know.

'Because,' Al said, 'for most supermarkets it's a race to the bottom, and that's where value engineering comes in. You want to sell your soup more cheaply? Then take out the more expensive ingredients or use fewer of them. Vegetable dyes and thickening – flour – will guarantee your mushroom soup looks like Company A's, and will have the same consistency. So now you can undercut their price.'

'But it won't taste as good,' Julia said.

Al laughed. 'That's where we come in. Find the right name for the brand, put it in big letters on the side of the carton, get an appropriate image, and you're away. "Nine out of Ten People Prefer Pickwick's Pea Soup".'

'So young and yet so cynical,' Martin said.

'It pays the rent.'

As the couple stood in the hall, about to leave for a late train, Julia asked him, 'Do you mind us calling you Al, or would you prefer Allen?'

'Albert's my full name,' he said, laughing, as he shrugged himself into his reefer jacket.

'Albert. You don't hear that much nowadays.' She hoped she sounded casual.

'It used to be a big name in Jamaica.'

Martin said, 'Is that where you were born?'

'No, but my Dad was. I'm a Londoner.' He held out his hand. 'Good to meet you,' he said, 'and many thanks for the meal.'

Julia wondered now, as she had often wondered since that first meeting, whether Polly and Al would marry. And if so, did they intend to raise a family? She hoped so, at all events if it would make Polly happy. But in reply to her oblique questions, Polly always said she was perfectly happy as she was. 'Early days,' she said, 'and I'm far too young to think about settling down. Besides, it's as much as Al and I can do to pay the rent on our shoebox of a flat.'

'And does Al think the same way?'

'Don't know,' Polly said. 'I've never asked him.'

Now, sitting on Polly's divan bed, Julia stared unseeing about her, thinking, Martin and I were married by her age. In fact, we were parents, *her* parents. And suddenly a great wave of grief overcame her and she began to cry, a series of gulping, shuddering sobs she couldn't control.

4

SHE'D THOUGHT SLEEP WOULD BE DIFFICULT, but as she sat sipping breakfast juice, Julia, despite a lengthy shower not yet fully awake, accepted that she had in fact passed an entirely untroubled, and as far as she could recall, dreamless night. The previous evening's unlooked for storm of tears seemed to belong to a different person. Today she had work to do.

And yet, standing at the kitchen sink as she rinsed out her glass, she thought, that *was* me. Why did I weep last night? The memory of a poem she had read as an undergraduate stirred in her brain – but it wasn't Keats she was recalling. Tears, idle tears. Gathering together the papers she needed for college, she knew which poem was coming to mind, but before she could turn its rhythm into words, the phone rang.

'Julia?' Martin's voice travelled across the world, clear and strong.

'I'm fine,' she said, then, realising how odd her words must sound, given that she had given him no opportunity to ask, added 'since you'll want to know.' That, too, sounded wrong. She tried again. 'I've only just had breakfast. How about you?'

'It's the middle of the night where I am. Breakfast is no more than a distant memory.' He was laughing but she could imagine his bewildered expression. 'What's the matter? You sound almost hysterical.'

'I need to tell you that Polly and Al are off to France for two weeks,' she said, gabbled almost. But as she spoke the words they began to calm her and, breathing more evenly, she reported their daughter's telephone call, Polly's evident delight at the prospect of her French holiday, one during which she and Al would share the driving, would go wherever the fancy took them. 'And Polly's promised to keep in touch. And of course she made me promise to pass on her love and to hope you'll enjoy your month in California.'

'I don't think there's much doubt of that.' And Martin spent several minutes on the sights and sounds he'd already experienced – including a couple of journeys by tram and a boat tour round part of the Bay which took him under the Bay Bridge. 'I'll keep you posted,' he told her. 'And I'll phone you in a couple of days' time. You've got my number if there's any emergency.'

'I'm fine,' she said again. 'Take care and have fun. And make sure the audiences for your lectures are a success.'

On the bus into town, she replayed their conversation. Awkwardness, the awkwardness of two people separated by thousands of miles, had finally given way to the shared familiarity of that anecdote about Oscar Wilde, one they so often repeated to each other. 'What of your new play, Mr Wilde. Will it prove a success, do you think?' 'Madame, the play is already a success. It remains to be seen whether the audience is equally successful.'

But – 'I'm fine.' What on earth prompted her to blurt those words out to Martin? She'd had no inkling of speaking them when his voice came down the line, and they'd startled her almost as much as they must have discomposed him.

She was still brooding over the remark when she got to college. In the foyer she came across the Principal pinning up notices, and called out a good morning.

'My,' Janine Hamilton said, as she turned from her task, and looked keenly at Julia. 'Greek sun certainly agrees with you.'

'I hope you've taken some time away from college cares,' Julia said, knowing the question was expected of her, and knowing what the response would be.

'Very little chance of relaxation for me, I'm afraid. Committees of this, committees of that, days and nights given over to balancing the books, planning for a new year with diminished resources ... '

The Principal enjoyed dramatising her role.

'I'm sorry to hear that,' Julia said, smiling sympathetically, though fully aware that Janine had only just returned from a three-week Caribbean cruise. 'I've popped in to collect my teaching schedule.'

'You'll find it waiting for you in the Secretary's office,' the Principal said, dropping all pretence of familiarity. 'I'm afraid you've lost one class. Enrolment is down and protection of full-time lecturers has of course to be our first priority.' And she turned back to the notice board.

'Come.' The college secretary, a pompous man whose name Julia did her best never to remember, handed her a folder, saying as he did so, 'You have fewer hours this coming term. There is a notable lessening of interest among our clientele in the study of Literature.' He spoke as though accusing her of being personally responsible for this state of affairs.

'Janine told me that enrolment was down.'

He stared at her as though he disapproved of her temerity in suggesting she might be on first-name terms with the Principal. Lowering his gaze, he studied his fingernails for some moments before he spoke again. 'The times are, I regret to say, unpropitious.' He raised his eyes, looked solemnly at her. 'There will be a full meeting of staff at the end of next week, before the teaching year commences. You will find the details in your folder.'

'I don't expect I'll get paid for my attendance?'

His look was intended as a reproof, his shrug a means of dismissing her presumption. You are a hired menial, the shrug said.

'And you're a prat,' she longed to tell him. But she left without speaking.

***

Walking up the drive to her front door she was greeted by her elderly next-door neighbour who, on all fours, was prodding at a flower bed beside the low hedge that divided the two properties. 'Your husband got off, alright, then?'

'Yes.' Julia stepped across the strip of lawn as the old woman clambered slowly to her feet and, trowel in one gloved hand, massaged her back with the other. 'Martin and I have spoken twice. Now he's over his jet lag he's ready to enjoy California.'

'I expect you'll be glad to have him back, safe and sound.'

'He's only just gone,' Julia said, laughing.

'My David's been gone getting on for six years, but I still miss him.' She paused, peered about her as if she was trying to locate her dead husband. 'I still talk to him every day.' Then, training her thick spectacles on Julia she said, 'If you're ever lonely, come round, won't you? Bang on the door. I'm a bit hard of hearing, but I can make us a cuppa and we'll have a chat.'

Digging her door key out of her bag, Julia said, 'That's kind of you.'

But standing in the front room and looking at the chair in which Martin often sat of an evening, she remembered how, days after Polly had first brought Al to meet her parents, the woman, who had seen them as they arrived, asked about the 'Black Chap', wanting to know whether he was 'going' with Polly, the foreboding in her voice overriding the attempt at polite enquiry, and she doubted she'd take up her neighbour's offer. Not that Martin and she hadn't been momentarily startled when Polly told them beforehand that Al's parents were Jamaican, but, as Martin said, 'So long as he isn't a crook or a wife-beater ...'

'Or a Tory.'

'Or an Arsenal supporter.'

Al, it turned out, wasn't interested in football. The only sport he enjoyed was squash, which he and Polly played – 'to win,' she said, as the four of them sat down to a meal Julia and Martin had prepared between them. 'Al does, anyway. He sulks forever if I take a game off him.'

Al laughed. 'You mean I would if you did.'

She punched him lightly in the ribs. 'I let you win, you know that.'

'Dream on,' Al said, leaning over to kiss her on the cheek.

Later that evening, after Polly had phoned to announce that she and Al were staying the night in Abbeville and that the following day they'd head on south – 'we'll phone again in a few days' time, probably from somewhere like Aix-en-Provence' – Julia opened her work folder onto the breakfast bar where she'd made herself eat a supper of soup and salad, and drew out the folder's contents. The top sheet of paper, intended for would-be students (*Copy to all Members of Staff*) trumpeted in large type the college's Mission Statement. To provide a learning experience in a competitive but creatively co-operative atmosphere in which outcomes could be monitored in accordance with client need. Courses were carefully structured with a view to maximising the successful achievement of aims and objectives and were progressed by a keenly motivated teaching staff.

Reading this, Julia thought of Martin's explosion of rage when he was first asked to commit to paper the aims and objectives of all the courses he taught. 'Pay-day for ships' lawyers,' he said. 'I give Joe Bloggs poor marks for writing sub-literate essays which demonstrate incomprehension, ignorance, and, very probably non-attendance, and Joe Bloggs sues the university for not making clear the aims and objectives of his courses and for bad teaching.'

'Really?'

'Really. Still, it's easy enough to avoid. Give everyone good marks. That way they don't complain. Why would they?'

'You mean a student can get a good degree for doing no work? But that's ridiculous.'

'No,' Martin said, 'it shows how brilliant the teaching is. The suits have got it worked out.'

'And who are the suits?' Julia had asked.

'People like Giles, I'm afraid,' Martin said, with gloomy relish. 'The kind of person for whom a degree in Business Studies was invented. Universities used to be places full of students and their tutors, with a few administrators to look after the day-to-day running of the place. Remember? Now each and every university is full of men and women in smart suits, all of them speaking the same jargon and all of them keen to show the place would fall apart without them. Hirers and firers. Administrators used to exist for the sake of universities. Now universities exist for the sake of administrators.'

'What about the students?'

'They aren't students,' Martin said, 'they're clients. Or customers, I forget which. But we aren't allowed to forget that, whether clients or customers, they have to be satisfied. Of course they do. They've paid good money, they expect good degrees. If they think they mightn't get them at University X they take their money to University Z. Demand and supply.'

Despite his penchant for exaggeration, there was, she knew from her own experience at college, truth in what Martin said. On the other hand, and as his paid-for month in San Francisco demonstrated, what he called half-derisively the world of higher learning still brought its rewards. No such luck for the lowly FE teacher.

Abruptly, she stood up and left the kitchen. Stop brooding. She went upstairs, running through her head the closing lines of *Paradise Lost* which she'd soon enough be discussing with her A Level class.

The world was all before them, where to choose
Their place of rest, and Providence their Guide.
They, hand in hand, with wandering steps and slow,
Through Eden took their solitary way.

My solitary way? No, I have Martin, hand in hand. She opened the door of the room across the landing from Polly's, Martin's study, peered around at the packed shelves of his books. Serried ranks, she thought, and then, speaking the words aloud, 'Serried? What *exactly* does that mean?'

Above Martin's desk was his two-volume *Oxford English Dictionary*. She took down Volume 2, N-Z and found the word she needed. 'Serried: **1**(Of soldiers etc.) pressed close together, shoulder to shoulder; *gen.* arranged in close-packed rows or lines. **2** Of argument, etc: closely reasoned, compact in expression.' Well, she thought, I've never come across anyone referring to a serried argument. Perhaps I'll try it out on Martin. Tell him that an argument of his isn't sufficiently serried. And she smiled to think of his puzzled expression.

She was about to close the book when she saw a scrap of what looked like notepaper poking out from beneath the page next to the one she'd been looking at. She drew the paper out, unfolded it. Cheap, pale blue, probably torn from a letter pad, it was folded in two. Presumably Martin had used it as a marker or in order to make a note, to record the meaning of a word by which he'd been stumped. She read the few words hastily scrawled across the page. At first she didn't understand their meaning.

And then, suddenly, she did.

II

5

'NATIONALITY?'

'British.'

The manager peered at the card he had given Julia to complete. 'This address, it is not British.'

'I live in Greece most of the year.'

'You have a passport?'

She reached into her bag, handed it over while trying to control her shaking hand, and, when he looked up at her from having studied her photograph, stared unsmilingly back into his dark eyes. Shorter than her, his sallow complexion and slender moustache suggested Mediterranean parentage.

'Born in Manchester I see. You have been in Greece for long?'

Yes, she thought, he was probably Spanish. 'Several years,' she said. 'I'm a teacher – and translator.'

'Ah, you are here for a conference, perhaps? We have many conferences in Brighton.'

'A few days' holiday, that's all.'

His nod suggested disappointment. The hotel would not be welcoming conferees. 'And you wish to pay, by how?'

'Cash,' she said.

Resting both hands on the reception desk as though to bolster his authority, he announced, 'Cash must be paid in advance.'

'Of course.' She took out her wallet, counted out two hundred pounds. 'This is for four nights,' she said, reaching for her bag. 'If I decide

43

to stay for longer I'll let you know.'

The manager drew a fountain pen from his waistcoat. 'Wait please, I must give you a receipt.'

His signature was an expansive flourish. 'First floor, room number fourteen,' he said, handing her a plastic card. 'This will open your door. You know how to insert it?' He came out from behind the desk, dapper in his dark suit, though his shoes she saw were of old cracked black leather. 'The lift is here.' He gestured towards a corner of the hotel foyer, where, beside the inevitable large potted plant, was a recessed door.

'I'll make my own way up,' she said. 'I don't like lifts.'

Minutes later, having unpacked and hung the very few clothes she'd brought with her, she stood at her window looking down at the thronged sunlit street, at couples dawdling before shop windows, most of them in shorts or jeans and T-shirts, as though fresh from or on their way to the beach. That was hidden from her view, though over the rooftops she could see a pale strip of sea fading into afternoon sky. Her breathing was by now returning to normal. Why had the manager stared at her as though she was not who she said she was, as though he had good reason to suspect her of being an imposter, a fraud, someone trying to hide a guilty secret? Damn him. Damn herself for being made so nervous. She *was* a teacher, and the tan from her recent month on the island made plausible her claim that she lived the year round in Greece. Not that it mattered. She was what she said – or she wasn't. As long as she paid for her stay what business was it of his who she was or what she did?

Watching a flight of gulls squabbling in mid-air over food scraps some had snatched up from street bins, she realised she was hungry.

In the small but surprisingly well-set up bathroom, she splashed cold water over her face before burying it some moments in the white bath towel – its bleach-and-pine scent was reassuringly impersonal – and then, pausing to look in the bedroom's full-length mirror and, after some hesitation, deciding the pale trousers and jacket she'd travelled in would do, picked up her shoulder bag and took herself back downstairs.

The hotel foyer, cooled by invisible air-conditioning, was empty. But as soon as she stepped outside the warmth of the September afternoon struck against her skin. Not the energy-sapping heat of Greece, but sufficient for her to relax into as she strolled the length of the street before turning off into what seemed an older part of the town, a tangle of narrow lanes, of bars, cafés, small restaurants. At this time of the day most were empty, some closed – late lunchers having departed, early diners not yet due – and she wandered through the lanes for some twenty minutes before finally choosing to enter one of the smaller cafés, the interior requiring her to adjust to its cool gloom before she chose a table from which she could, if she wished, watch the passers-by.

A young woman in black T-shirt and black jeans came to take her order. Carrot cake and coffee – Americano. No, no milk. The woman nodded. 'No probs' she said, and went to fulfil the order.

Taking from her jacket pocket the book she'd brought with her, Julia turned to the poem she'd read on the train coming down and re-read the lines that had forced themselves on her attention.

> We'll stay home, light fires, drink wine and put the times to right
> In song. Don't see this as failure or withdrawal from the world.
> There's honesty, truth in what you do. Though reason proves
> Love deceives at every turn, hands back the ring, breaks every vow
> Still our actions are compelled by it. It's all we own.

The title of the poem was given as 'XXX'. Not, she thought, three kisses, but the Latin for thirty, suggesting that this was a translation from a Roman poet, though kisses might be an ironic element in the poem's meaning. 'Watch as new buds break,' it ended, 'Candles lit / To guide the hungry lover home to love – hair unbound, his face, / Turning the corner where trees vault the road, besotted with green.'

'Hair unbound'. You wouldn't use such a phrase about a modern lover, would you, not even a hippy of the kind the town she was in seemed to have in large numbers, their faces not so much besotted with green as hairy, wild with whiskers.

But in a sense you could think of them as green men. Young, the sap pulsing through them, and, yes, wild, untamed. Or, of course, as callow as they were probably malodorous, in need of a good scrub down, so her no-nonsense mother might have said. She shut the book. She was becoming ridiculous, a fifty-year-old woman alone in a southern town, flying loose of her moorings, gone from home and its friendly hearthside. Don't see this as failure? If not, then what?

Her coffee and cake arrived and at once she wished she'd asked for something more substantial. But when the woman asked as a matter of routine whether that would be all, Julia merely nodded. A bill was left beside her plate.

Alone, she looked about her. Withdrawal from the world. Yes, that about summed it up. She forked carrot cake into her mouth, swallowed almost without tasting, and drank her coffee in a couple of gulps. Having glanced at the bill, she dug into her purse for the right money plus tip, stood up and went out, pulling the door shut as though she was closing something off.

***

As she crossed the hotel foyer, the hotel manager, an elbow either side of the ledger he had open on the reception desk, looked up. 'Good afternoon, madam,' he said, his smile one of ready welcome. 'How may I help you, please?' Then the smile changed to a frown of concentration, more, perhaps, a slight pucker of the eyebrows as he tried to remember who she was.

'Number fourteen,' she said.

'Of course.' The smile returned. 'Will madam be dining with us tonight? The restaurant is open from six o'clock until ten each weekday.'

'I think I'll eat out,' she said.

'Very well, madam.' He ducked back to studying the ledger. She was dismissed.

Julia took the stairs up to her room, pulled the curtains shut against the still-bright afternoon, and, fully dressed, lay on her bed.

When she woke the room was in darkness. She felt for the switch to the bedside lamp and looked at her watch. Nearly half-past ten. She had been asleep for rather more than five hours and it was now too late to go in search of a meal. She lay on her back and stared at the ceiling. Don't see this as failure or withdrawal from the world.

6

NEXT MORNING, EARLY, HAVING OPENED HER curtains to another blue day, she ran a bath, determined to soak away the sad emptiness of the previous twenty-four hours, and resolved on activities to come. A vigorous morning walk to begin with. Among the sheaf of papers she had found in her room's imitation leather folder, including a coloured street map advertising PLACES OF HISTORICAL INTEREST, GOOD DINING, and, of course, YOUR SHOPPING NEEDS CATERED FOR, was one that gave instructions for out-of-town picturesque trails. Good. And good that after lunch she could spend time in the Dome's museum and picture gallery. She climbed from the bath, and towelling her freshly-washed hair, told herself she felt re-invigorated.

But once in the restaurant she felt both conspicuous and awkward. A girl who looked impossibly young in her black dress and white frilly apron stood by the door to ask her room number. 'This is a self-service restaurant,' the girl said, her voice little more than a whisper. 'Sit anywhere you like. Someone will come to take your order for choice of beverage.'

As most of the tables were already occupied anywhere you like turned out to be at the far end of the restaurant and about as far from anything Julia liked as she could imagine, especially as it required her to pass by numbers of business-suited men who broke off their talk when she passed their tables in order to stare openly at the middle-aged woman dressed in dark blue blouse and jeans who was on her own. And when she finally arrived at the table she was supposed to like, it was to discover that it was cluttered with dirty crockery and that a crumpled napkin lay on the chair where she was to sit.

She picked the napkin up between thumb and first finger, dropped it on the table, and sat down to wait. A man at the next table, who had paused in tapping away at his laptop to watch, leant over and said 'You're supposed to get your own brekker, love. Better hurry while there's some left.' He jerked his head in the direction of trestle-tables on which Julia could see cups, plates, bowls, and, beside them a row of large silver dishes and jugs of what, as she tried them, proved to be milk and hot water.

As for the dishes, they held strips of pink, raw-looking bacon which she rejected at a glance as she did the sad-eyed fried eggs.

Digging uncertainly into a pallid mound of scrambled egg from which water leaked thinly, she watched a white-shirted arm reach past her and a voice, loud, falsely hearty, said 'If you're not having the bacon ... '

She turned to face a jowled, red-faced man, his stomach forcing apart the lower buttons of his shirt, trousers strained against his thighs.

'Now then, Roger,' another voice said. 'Show some restraint. Ladies first.' The speaker, standing at Roger's shoulder, smirked at her as he said, 'No manners, I'm afraid. They didn't teach them at the school my friend went to. Borstal, that was.' And he opened his mouth to laugh, teeth, some chipped, all discoloured, connected by a thread of spittle.

Julia carried the plate back to her now cleared table and as she sat, her neighbour, in the act of closing his laptop, said, 'Pays to get in early, love. The lot who eat here' – another jerk of the head – 'they'll hoover up whatever's on offer.' He stood and as he did so glanced down at her scrambled egg. 'Yeah, I had that, too. Well down to their usual standard.' And he left.

After several minutes, during which she had tried and then left virtually uneaten the plate of congealed egg, and chewed through a piece of limp toast, a girl who looked even younger than the one who had greeted Julia, came up to her. 'Tea or coffee?' she asked. She, too, spoke in a whisper.

'Is the coffee fresh ground?'

The question seemed to daze the girl. 'It's what they all have,' she finally said.

'In that case,' Julia said, 'I'll have tea.'

* * *

But three hours of walking in the sun, the wind on the downs sufficient to cool her skin even as it riffled her hair and whispered about her ears, brought her calm of mind, of equanimity, all passion spent. Reaching a bench near cliff-tops high above the sea, she sat, sprawled rather, content to let her gaze wander about the vastness of sky and then drop to consider the sea shimmering far below. 'The deep blue air,' she thought, 'that shows Nothing, and is nowhere, and is endless.' She looked about her but she had the place to herself. Aloud, she repeated, 'Don't see this as failure or withdrawal from the world.' And then, more loudly, 'And don't be such a self-pitying wimp', adding words familiar to her from childhood, 'There's plenty worse off than you.'

She stood briskly up and began the walk over tussocky grass down to a road from where, the Hotel Guide informed her, she could catch a bus back to town.

Some forty or so minutes later, still glowing from her physical exertion, thirsty and in need of food, she was sitting in a small café. Not the one she'd favoured the previous afternoon, though this one, too, was in a narrow lane strung with bars and restaurants, and she'd chosen it because it looked less showy than most and, she hoped, would therefore be less expensive. The café was far from empty, but she spotted an unoccupied table towards the rear and made her way to it. Once there, back to the counter, she picked up the menu and saw at a glance that the café's subfusc appearance was no guarantee of modest pricing. What could she afford? The insufficient breakfast followed by her long tramp had left her hungry but she had to be careful not to spend out of the money she'd brought from home.

'Are you ready to order?'

The voice, that of a young man, came from above and behind her. Still looking at the menu, she said slowly, as though after consideration, 'I think I'll have the chef's salad and a glass of white wine.'

'Sauvignon? Pinot Grigio?'

'House white will be fine,' Julia said turning to the waiter. Then, 'Good God. Orlando.'

'Mrs Gibbs.' Orlando looked as taken aback, embarrassed even, as she felt. In what seemed habitual waiter's garb of black T-shirt and black jeans, he loomed, tall, angular, though his hair was tied in a pony-tail and he seemed to have trimmed his straggle of beard. His smile uncertain, he asked, 'Are you here on holiday?'

Meaning that he assumed her holiday began and ended in Greece.

'I'm here for a very few days,' she said, adding by way of explanation and to close off speculation, 'to look around. Then it's back to work.' How stupid her words must seem.

Orlando said, as though to help her, 'Oh, of course, Professor Gibbs is in America.' But even in the dim light of the café she could see that he realised this remark might well be a gaffe.

'I'm on my own,' she said, which was no better.

Orlando looked anxiously around, and 'Coming' he called, perhaps in relief, to a man a few tables away who was waving for attention. To Julia, and speaking formally, he said, 'I'll attend to your order as soon as I've dealt with that table's bill.' And he went.

A few minutes later, during which she wondered at herself, he was back with her glass of wine and cutlery which he arranged in front of her, saying as he did so, 'I imagine you prefer retsina but this isn't bad.'

He watched as she took a sip of wine.

'No, not retsina,' Julia agreed. 'But, as you say, not bad either.'

'Phew.' He made a show of mopping his brow.

Laughing, feeling now less ill-at-ease, Julia said 'I was going to ask what you were doing here, but of course you were a student at the local university, weren't you.' She looked enquiringly at him. Help me out here.

He held up his hands in mock surrender. Got me bang to rights.

Again, she laughed. 'Didn't your father say that you and some friends were hoping to start a community newspaper?'

'We still are.' He was looking around, keen to demonstrate his waiterly attentiveness. But he turned back, smiling. 'Waiting pays the rent while we're at the planning stage,' he said. Then he left her.

Hands folded, she stared down at the table. Suppose Orlando told Giles of his unlooked-for meeting with Julia Gibbs? But somehow she doubted whether he would. Anyway, for all she knew Orlando's work was something he'd choose to keep silent about. It wasn't so much that he feared parental disapproval as that, to judge at least from what had passed between father and son on the island a few weeks back, he was indifferent to whatever Giles might think or say. She was on Orlando's side in the matter, and besides, here, in this café, he seemed quite different from the petulant youth of Greece, amusing, at his ease, and, within limits, friendly. So when he brought her salad, she said, blurting the words out, 'It would be nice to talk at leisure.' And, by way of explanation, of justification, of apology, 'I'm sure you can tell me about some of the places I should visit while I'm here. This is my first visit.' A small, intendedly self-deprecatory laugh. 'If you can bear to be seen with an old lady, that is.'

She hoped he hadn't noticed the blush that she was certain accompanied the sudden heat spreading up her neck to her face. What on earth had induced her to use such words? But to her surprise, he said 'Yes, I'd like that.' Though as if not wanting to be overheard, he said, lowering his voice, 'I'm free this evening.'

'Purely by chance, so am I,' she said, laughing to cover the acute embarrassment she now felt. 'Coffee house? Bar?'

'Bar,' Orlando said, and with swift certainty, 'There's a place further along this lane that's OK. The G and B.' No doubt in response to her mystified look, he added, 'Gin and Beer? Girls and Boys? Good and Bad? Your guess is as good as mine. But the natives are friendly.'

'I'm happy to believe you,' she said, breathing more evenly. 'What time?'

'Dunno. Eight o'clock?'

'Eight o'clock it is,' she said. And, as she took a mouthful of wine then began to fork up her salad, she felt, for the first time in days, a faint but unmistakeable stirring within her, a discernible lift, a lightening of the grey mood that had settled on her.

7

BUT LATER, BACK IN HER HOTEL, Julia lay on the bed wondering at herself. What on earth had possessed her to make that invitation to meet Orlando for an evening drink? Had he meant it when he said 'I'd like that'? Unlikely. More likely he had nothing to do or was already seeing the chance of an anecdote he could share with giggling friends. 'There was this woman, old enough to be my mother, who tried to pick me up in the café, arranged to meet me for a drink at G and B.' And then one of his mates saying, 'Sounds like a right old slapper. Pay you, did she?' followed by guffaws all round.

She shuddered. And yet, she thought, Orlando's pleasure at her suggestion – one she'd had no idea she would utter, it had come as a complete surprise – seemed genuine enough. And after all why *couldn't* they meet for a friendly drink? They knew each other, she was an old acquaintance of his father's ... Oh, god, suppose he *did*, after all, mention it to Giles. 'I met your friend Julia, in Brighton. She was on her own, seemed a bit at a loose end. She took me for a drink.' 'On her own, eh?' She could hear Giles's fruity voice, the note of roguish enquiry. Julia, a free woman on the rampage ... Well, of course, at her age ...

It wasn't as if she could ask Orlando to keep quiet about their meeting. That would be ... Well, what *would* it be? Her husband was away, in America, she was a free agent, entitled to go wherever she wanted, wasn't she? She didn't have to account to casual acquaintances for her every action. Besides, even if Orlando was on better terms with Giles than seemed the case when they were all on the island, the two weren't likely to be in regular touch. It wasn't how relationships between parents and adult offspring worked. She loved Polly devotedly, thought her daughter returned at least a fair measure of that love, but they rarely spoke more often than once a week, by phone; and they saw each other far less frequently. No, be sensible. Orlando wouldn't be rushing to tell his father about his fortuitous encounter with Julia Gibbs. Anyway, what was there to tell? Nothing. Nothing bar the fact that the wife of Giles's oldest friend had turned up in Brighton. And again she heard Giles's voice. '*Brighton?* Rather off limits, surely?'

Oh, shut up. She felt her eyelids droop. The vigorous morning walk, her lunchtime glass of wine, were combining to make her drowsy. She rolled on her side, not so much deciding on as submitting to a short nap.

But when she jerked awake and looked at her watch she found it was half-past six. She'd slept for longer than she'd intended. Time for a wash and brush-up, as her father used to say, and then dress for the evening. She swung her legs off the bed, stood, stretched, and only then remembered how she would be spending the evening.

Standing in the bath she let the shower attachment play over her, enjoying the feel of warm water cascading over her bare flesh. When she stepped out she wiped the misted-up mirror with her towel, studied her face, turning it this way and that. No hiding those threads of grey hair among the blonde, the beginnings of a sagging jaw line, the deepening grooves either side of her nose. She lifted her fringe, looked at the crease lines along her forehead, said to herself, disparagingly and perhaps self-protectingly, you're no spring chicken, my love, and quickly completed the task of drying her body.

Once she was dressed, in a fresh blouse and a long denim skirt, she wondered about tights. No, her brown, strappy sandals looked well enough with bare legs still tanned from a month's exposure to Greek sun. Sitting at the mirror-stool she began to apply eye-shadow and a touch of lipstick, but, having looked in the glass, she rubbed at her lips until they were free of artificial colour. 'The eyes have it,' she said aloud, and winked at her image. No spring chicken, but hens can party. The thought made her feel slightly hysterical.

Half-past seven, her watch told her. The walk to the place of –

assignation, should she call it? – would, she estimated, take twenty minutes. Time, soon, to move. She got up, began to pace about her room, as she so often did reciting to herself poems she kept in her memory's store-cupboard. Then, noticing the telephone on her bedside table, she sat down beside it, reached in her bag for her address book, and then phoned room service. Could she have an outside line? She could, and it would be added to her bill. Oh, she'd paid in advance. Then perhaps madam would care to settle up with the management at an early opportunity, and in the meantime she was at liberty to use her phone to contact the outside world. 'Thank you,' she said, and dialled the number she wanted.

It rang out and then clicked to answer phone. 'There is nobody here right now to answer your call. Please leave a name and number and we'll get back to you as soon as possible. Please speak after the tone.'

'This is Julia Gibbs,' Julia said, 'Hoping to speak to Trudy Cosgrove. It is now twenty to eight on Wednesday evening and I am about to go out, but I should be back by ten o'clock and I will try again then. I hope you're well.' She was about to break the connection but then changed her mind and again lifted the receiver to her lips. 'I'd very much like to speak to you,' she said.

Then she left.

***

But though she walked slowly across town, pausing every so often to look in shop windows, she reached the bar a minute or two before eight o'clock. Would Orlando be there already? She hesitated to step inside but the door suddenly swung open and a couple emerged into the evening sunlight, laughing, happy, but not so absorbed in each other for the man, a mere youth he seemed, to neglect to hold the door for the middle-aged woman who, standing uncertainly outside, had no alternative but to smile acceptance of his gesture and enter the G and B.

In the cool gloom, Julia looked around her, took in the few couples sitting at tables or sprawling along banquettes. Then she walked across to the bar.

The barman, tall, with a wispy goatee and blond hair styled, she supposed, in imitation of, or homage to, some rock star – or might it be sportsman? – waited silently for her to speak. Her request for a small glass of Pinot Grigio was greeted with a nod, the drink was placed in front of her, she handed over a five pound note and in exchange received two twenty pence coins, and she was free to go.

Go where? An empty table near the door seemed best. That was she could escape if, as now seemed likely, Orlando failed to appear. She would give him fifteen minutes at most and then leave. She should never have come. A woman on her own in a bar where the average age of other drinkers was, at a guess, somewhere below thirty, what else was she to feel but scalded by isolation?

'Mind if I join you?'

The man hovering at the table, white haired, bent shoulders, was wearing what in the bar's uncertain light looked to be an old dark grey jacket and brown cords. His scrawny neck poked out of a thin, white sweater and he was smiling uncertainly, eyes anxious behind thick spectacles.

So I'm a pick up for the graveyard brigade, Julia thought, savagely. She shrugged without speaking but he took this as sufficient invitation to drop into the seat facing her.

Raising a small tumbler filled with colourless liquid, he said, 'Water. It's all I'm allowed.' He drank, made a wry grimace. 'Just out of hospital, that's me.' He shook his head, as if in wonderment. 'One minute I'm OK, the next I'm in an ambulance off to A&E. Been there all day, can you believe, being looked over by the men in white coats. I've only just got out,' he said again, this time as if he could scarcely believe it.

Oh, god, she thought, I'm in the company of a lunatic. Curse you, Orlando.

'It was the pain in my leg, that's what did it. Terrible. They had to call an ambulance. I've been there all day. Turned out to be a blood clot. Got given this stuff, warfarin, rat poison, can you believe it?'

She forced herself to look at him, saw the fear in his expression, heard the faint desperation in his words. 'I'm sorry,' she said. Then, 'Who called the ambulance?'

'Two of the men at work. I'd only just got in, too. I run a paper re-cycling plant, see.' The words seemed to spur him to further explanation. 'It's a good little business, mind. We get paper sent us, we bale it up, load it onto lorries, off it goes to Liverpool docks, onto a container ship, and across the seas. Guess where it ends up? China.' He shook his head in wonder. 'Bloody great factories, these container ships, by the time one of them gets to Shanghai all the paper's been turned into cardboard. Bloody amazing. The Chinese use a lot of cardboard.'

He drank most of the water, toyed with his glass, and said, 'I'll tell you something else. My brother, he ran his own business, making roof insulation. Bet you can't guess what the insulation material's made of.' He leant across the table and Julia saw that his eyes had now quite lost their anxious, fretful look, and were gleaming with anticipation of what he was about to tell her.

Obligingly, she shook her head. 'No idea.'

'Body parts,' he said. 'True as I sit here. Placenta, that kind of thing.'

Before she could think what to say, he added, 'Mind, he died some years back, and the business died with him.' He paused, looked at her. 'I don't want that to happen to me,' he said emphatically. He drained his glass. 'I mean we've all got to go, but I want to leave something to the kids.' The doleful expression was back. 'To be straight with you, I don't even know if they'll be grateful. Left home years ago, the pair of them, went off to Australia. Haven't seen them since they came to their mother's funeral and that was the best part of six years ago.'

Julia felt compelled to speak. 'Haven't you wanted to go to see them?'

He shrugged. 'Don't know they'd be all that keen to see me. We were never close. I was off most of the time they were growing up, see, working away from home, overseas half the time. It was the wife who had the care of them.' He looked at her, his expression remorseful, was it, or merely blank? This is how life can be. 'You got kids?'

'A daughter.'

'Husband still living?'

She knew what the question implied. Why are you on your own?

'Yes,' she said. 'My husband's still living.'

He stood. 'Lucky for some,' he said. 'Well, nice talking to you.' He looked round the bar, fuller now than it had been when, twenty minutes earlier, Julia had arrived.

'Can I get you another drink?' he asked, looking at her near-empty glass.

Julia shook her head. 'No thanks. I'm about to leave myself.'

But as he turned away and she made to rise she saw Orlando come bursting through the door.

He saw her at once, strode across. 'Sorry,' he said, 'Very, very sorry.' He drew breath. 'A bit of a row about the newspaper. Advertising. How to share the leg work.'

'I'm *so* sorry,' Julia said with satiric intent. But for all that, she was, she accepted, relieved to see him. She hadn't, after all, been stood up.

8

AS JULIA WALKED BACK TO HER hotel, alone, the ten o'clock chimes were sounding along the town's crowded streets. She had refused Orlando's offer to accompany her, an offer made, she was pretty sure, out of politeness rather than a desire to prolong their talk – she had seen the discreet glances he directed at his watch and guessed he was planning to go on to a meeting with others, perhaps a girlfriend. Besides, in the warm night air she was content to be on her own, steering her way round clusters of pedestrians, some hurrying to pub or bar, others, usually in twos and threes, sauntering arm in arm or pressed close to each other as they passed her, seemingly without registering her presence. A *flâneuse*, that's what she was. Then, remembering with a sudden lurch of embarrassment a moment earlier that evening, she amended the term to *fiery flâneuse*.

She was still thinking about that when she reached her hotel and was greeted by the manager, who seemed forever on duty. Had she enjoyed a pleasant evening? Yes, she was happy to say that she had. The manager was delighted to hear that; he wished her a good night's sleep, adding that should she require room service, she might like to note that it operated through the night, but that small extra charges were made for services provided between the hours of midnight and six a.m.

What services? she wondered, as she climbed the stairs to her room. 'I wish to order a young man, please, complete with champagne on ice.' Suppose she had brought Orlando back with her? No, don't be silly. But he had been agreeable company. And again, she recalled the moment when she'd seen in his eyes a flicker of – of what, contrition? Mute understanding? Yes, she thought, that was it.

It had come when, as they sat opposite each other exchanging trivial, polite, strained chit-chat – 'How was your day?', 'How was yours?', 'Why does a barman say "It's no problem" when you order a drink, as though finding a drink in a bar *might* be a problem?'– he had paused in the middle of some inconsequential anecdote about a pair of difficult customers who kept changing their minds about what food they wanted and was, she realised, listening to the music that came softly enough from the bar's sound system. '"Richard Cory",' he said, with an apologetic shrug of his shoulders. 'Old stuff, but I like it.' And, presumably seeing her look of puzzlement, said, 'Simon and Garfunkel. Though I guess you know that.'

'It may be their song,' she said, 'but the words aren't theirs.' And when he looked questioningly at her, she added, 'It's a poem. By Edwin Arlington Robinson.'

'Who's he? The husband of Mrs Robinson?'

'Very funny.' She put her hands together in a gesture of pretend approval. 'But this Robinson never married. He was a loner, like most of the people he wrote about. Richard Cory may have been a man of means but he ended up, didn't he, putting a bullet through his head? Now, why did he do that?'

He took some time to reply. 'I suppose *because* he was a man of means,' he said. 'The rich are lonely.'

'Possibly,' she said, 'though that sounds very sixtyish, don't you think? "Let's cancel the sounds of silence, good people, by getting it on and all coming together. Empty pockets and full hearts. Love rules."' She looked quizzically at him, a smile of reproof, she knew, on her lips. 'But in Robinson's world everyone is lonely.' And she quoted to him the last lines of a poem she knew by heart:

> There was not much that was ahead of him,
> And there was nothing in the town below,
> Where strangers would have shut the many doors
> That many friends had opened long ago.

'What's that from?' he asked her, impressed.

'"Mr Flood's Party". It's a great poem – about a lonely old drunkard who climbs a hill with a jug of whisky and holds a party for himself.'

'I'd like to read it,' Orlando said. He lifted his glass, drank slowly, thoughtfully, and when he returned the now empty glass to the table was silent for a few moments while he looked around the now thronged and increasingly noisy bar before turning back to meet her gaze. 'But I don't understand why the townspeople would have closed their doors to the old man – to Flood.'

Julia wanted to slap him. 'The poem doesn't say that, Orlando. It's what Flood himself thinks. And not "closed" but *shut*. Can't you hear the difference?'

Orlando was looking at her, startled by the sudden vehemence of her words.

'Go on,' she ordered him. 'Say it. Say "closed".'

As though uncertain of her meaning, Orlando again looked round the room, and she realised from glances directed at them from nearby tables that her voice was louder than she'd intended.

'Closed,' he said, his voice little more than a whisper.

'Now say "shut".' She herself had lowered her voice, self-conscious now, aware that she must sound like a reproving scold.What was this, a lesson in elocution? Mother reproving son for not closing the door whenever he left home?

'Shut.' Orlando was definitely whispering now.

But it was good enough. Julia, recovering from her momentary loss of control, turned anger into a display of mock reproof. Teacher to backward pupil. 'You can hear the difference, surely?' She dropped her eyes, looked at her own near-empty glass, said, as if to herself, 'closed – ' letting her voice linger on the *o*, that long regretful, reluctant vowel. 'Shut.' She slammed her hand down on the table. 'Over in a second, brief, emphatic. *Bang*.' She fixed him with a stare. 'You don't say the door banged closed, do you? You say it banged shut. *That's* the difference. *That's* that sound of rejection. *That's* what Mr Flood fears.'

Orlando was staring frankly at her. In wonderment? Consternation? 'Yes,' he said after a moment. 'I *do* see.' Another moment's silence. He said, with evident sincerity, though he was smiling, 'If you don't mind my saying so, you'd make a great teacher.'

'I am a teacher,' she said. 'And I apologise for shouting.'

'It's no problem,' he said, laughing, mouth wide open so she could see how white his teeth were, the pink inner lips. 'Really. It's OK. I don't mind.' How young he was.

'And I don't mind buying us both another glass of wine,' she said, feeling a mild elation.

Mature woman seen in bar buying wine for young man. Son? Gigolo? Toy Boy? Think what you like, she said to herself as the barman, a slight smirk on the puffy lips that centred his goatee, served her. She paid, made a show of slowly and carefully counting the change he brought her, tipped the coins into her purse, pushed that into her jacket pocket, and then carried the glasses back to where Orlando was sitting, upright, the image of polite obedience. 'Kalo krasi,' she said, taking her seat, then sipping her wine.

'That means "good wine", doesn't it?' He looked puzzled. 'It's not what Greeks say.'

She leant towards him. 'Don't look now,' she said, 'but when you do I think you'll find we're not in Greece.' And she leant back with a conspiratorial wink.

She wondered whether he would think she was drunk, and was relieved when he said, laughing, 'Just what I was thinking.'

'Do you wish we were? I mean, were you sorry to leave?'

'No!' After a moment, he said, as though abashed by the energy with which he'd uttered the word, 'To be truthful, I was glad to get away. As you no doubt noticed, my father and I aren't getting on at all well.'

She waited for him to say more and when he didn't – he was staring into his drink as though embarrassed by the confession – she said, 'I suppose, fingers crossed, I've been lucky. Or perhaps mothers and daughters always get on better with each other than fathers and sons.'

He looked up now, frowning. 'Corin got out early,' he said. 'He couldn't stand our father's ... well, his ways of giving us to understand that he was the big white chief. Always was, always would be. Women – you must have noticed, or at least heard rumours. Not that it bothers our mother, at least I don't think it does. She's got her own life, jetting around the world, more often on the concert platform than at home. Well, good for her. Corin reckons the old man is jealous of her success.'

He looked as though he was about to say more, but stopped, again concentrating on his still-full glass.

Julia said, 'But Giles – your father – is a successful man, surely?'

'That's how he comes on,' Orlando said. He raised his head and she saw he was now determined to speak out. The increasing noise of the crowded bar meant they had to lean closer to hear each other's words. Even so, she missed his next sentence, had to ask him to repeat it.

More loudly, he said, 'All that screwing around. It's his way of proving he's Mr Irresistible.' Then, lowering his voice, so she had to strain to catch his words, he said, speaking with sardonic emphasis, 'It's not only her – our mother – he's jealous of. Know what he calls your husband? The famous Professor Gibbs.' He looked at her with a kind of shamefaced defiance.

Julia shrugged. 'If it's any satisfaction to your father,' she said, 'according to my husband all academic reputations die.' He certainly does not like his father, she thought.

And as if to confirm this, Orlando said, 'I can't believe you don't see through all the old pals act they put on once a year. Or perhaps the others aren't pretending. My father certainly is. That's why Corin never comes and I try to keep away. Can't stand it.'

'You came this summer.'

'I had debts. My father offered to pay them off if I'd agree to play Happy Families. "One last time." That was how he put it.'

'In that case,' Julia said with some asperity, 'I think you ought to have made more of an effort to please him.'

Orlando looked at her, nodded glumly, accepting the reproof. 'I know,' he said. 'I feel bad about that.' And after a moment, he added, 'I did apologise to him when we were on our own. And to be fair, he told me it didn't matter.'

'That was good of him.'

Orlando looked sharply at her, then, realising she intended no sarcasm, said, 'He has his virtues.' He shook his head, irritated with himself. 'That sounds wrong. I don't mean to condescend, and in a way I love him. He's generous and he can be good company. But I wish he'd stop all this ... ' He left the sentence unfinished. Lifting his glass, he emptied it in one swallow, said as he put it down, 'Corin reckons he's in competition with James whatsisname for the number of notches he can count on his bedpost.'

'James Piper isn't married,' Julia said. And after a moment, she added, 'Which may have its disadvantages. After all, he could end up like Mr Flood, a lonely old man.'

'But for now he's more like Richard Cory, isn't he?' Orlando said.

'Fluttering pulses, clean favoured and imperially slim,' Julia said.

'Was he always like that?'

'As far as I can remember,' Julia said. 'But it was all so long ago.'

The words, lightly enough spoken, weighed with a sudden heaviness, and she could say no more, sadness constricting her throat. I was once as young as this youth sitting opposite me, she thought, quick to judgement, ridiculous, no doubt, in my assured condemnations.

She drank the last of her wine, and stood abruptly up. 'I must go,' she said, when she had regained her composure and could once again speak.

Orlando, surprised by the suddenness of her movements, stood, too, but when he suggested he walk with her she was quick to shake her head. Extending her hand, she said, 'I don't suppose I'll see you again before I leave. I have to go back home on Sunday. Work beckons.'

He made no answer and as they lightly clasped hands, she said, with a return of the awkwardness their talk had for a while pushed away, 'Thank you for agreeing to this ... this evening. I've enjoyed it.' And before he could think of a reply, she turned and left. Let him not have to concoct words of polite kindness. She wanted no pity.

***

Having cleaned her teeth and undressed, she sat on the side of her bed half-listening to the street noises, the voices of loud, cheerful companionship, or, raucous in song, holiday-makers, locals out for a good time, students arriving at, or returning to, the university, variously drunk, joyous, belligerent, and she thought of her own student days. The words she had spoken half an hour earlier came back and with them a return of the emotion she'd felt when uttering them, the shock of sadness. It was all so long ago.

Thirty years since they had all first met. Then it had seemed so easy, the declarations of friendship, of intimate companionship, of, yes, judgement on others. They had been young. The words of a poem she liked came, unbidden, into her mind. 'Children picking up our bones, / Will never know that these were once / As quick as foxes on the hill.' Yes, she thought, we were, or liked to think we were, quick as foxes, full of darting, playful delight in each other's company. And now? Why *did* they all continue with these joint holidays on the island? What, apart from a few shared student years, did they have in common? Precious little was the honest answer. Perhaps what had brought about their renewed friendships, the insistence on the annual rite of meeting, was above all the desire to fashion links that could outlast the years. On more than one occasion, sitting at the beach taverna, she'd caught someone's eye – James, say, or Tessa – and known that they were thinking, as she was: *why are we here?* Yet year after year back they came, Giles more professionally affable, it seemed, each summer, and James seldom with the same partner, not all of the so-different women he introduced pleased to be part of the group, as they made plain, though Trudy seemed content with their company.

Trudy! She must try her again.

Within a few seconds of reception putting her through, the phone was picked up and Trudy's voice said, rather crossly Julia thought, 'Cosgrove.'

'Trudy. It's me, Julia Gibbs. Is this a bad time to call you?' Perhaps James was waiting to take her to bed.

'*Julia.* No, *of course* it's not too late.' Trudy's voice had changed from irritability to pleasure. 'I played back your message when I got in and tried contacting you, but without any luck. Did you know your phone was switched off?'

'My mobile? Yes. It still is.'

'Oh?'

'I'm not at home,' Julia said, increasing, no doubt, Trudy's curiosity.

'Oh?' Trudy said again. Then, after a pause, 'I see. Or rather I don't see. Do you mean ... ?' But she stopped as if she had no idea what Julia might mean, and in the pause, Julia said, 'I mean I left my phone behind.' She was silent for a moment. Then, unsure whether she should be revealing this, half-fearful, half-daring, 'I didn't want people to know where I was,' she said.

If she hoped, or feared, that Trudy might ask why, she was disappointed or, perhaps, reassured. Because as though ignoring her last remark – confession, declaration? – Trudy asked, 'And where exactly are you?'

'I'm in Brighton.'

'*Brighton?*' This time Trudy sounded less curious than startled. 'On your own?' Then she giggled. 'Sorry, that sounds improper, doesn't it?'

Julia said, 'No, it's alright. I am on my own. In a hotel. Though, would you believe, quite by chance I bumped into Orlando Poynter.'

'Giles's son? That grumpy sod. What did he do, run away? Take a swing at you?'

'I've just left him. We had a drink in a bar near to where he works.'

Trudy said, 'Look here, are you sure you're sober? Quite sober?'

'Quite sober,' Julia told her. Then, more swiftly, 'I'm leaving here on Sunday and I wondered whether on my way through London we could perhaps meet for an hour. Unless you have other plans. James ... ?'

'Oh, James and I have had a row. It ended with me telling him to shove off. When the phone rang I thought it might be him. So no, I have no other plans for Sunday.'

'Well, in that case,' Julia began but Trudy cut her off.

'Tell you what, Julia. Why don't I zip down to Brighton for a day? It only takes the blink of an eyelid from Victoria and Brighton's one of my favourite places. Sea, sand, and sex, as the posters say.'

'Not any of the posters I've seen.'

'You have to know where to look.'

'Anyway,' Julia said, 'you're a working girl, so that only leaves Saturday.'

'Saturday is spoken for, I'm afraid.'

'Well, then.' As quickly as elation had come to Julia, it went.

'But Friday is free. James has given me the day off. My guess is he's arranged a meeting with some bimbo.'

'Is that what you argued about?' Julia asked.

'Got it in one. Let me come to Brighton and I can tell you all about it.' She paused. Then she said, 'And you can tell me whatever's on *your* mind.'

Julia, sitting in her bedside chair, felt a sudden gust of panic hit her.

'Julia?'

'Here,' she said. Then, trying to control her voice, 'Yes, do come on Friday. I'd love that.'

'Julia,' Trudy said. 'Are you crying?' Her voice softened. 'You sound upset. What's the matter?'

'Nothing.' Julia waited until her breathing returned to normal. 'I ... I'll look up train times and phone you tomorrow. About this time?' Wiping her eyes with the back of her hand, she glanced at her watch. Nearly eleven o'clock.

'That will be fine,' Trudy said. 'Take care, Julia.' And she rang off.

Hunched on her chair, trying to control her weeping, Julia thought, I hardly know her and she's far younger than me, and yet ...

She sat up, went into the bathroom and splashed cold water on her face without looking in the mirror.

As she lay in the dark, waiting for sleep to overtake her, street cries gradually fading, she wondered how much she would want to tell Trudy when they met on Friday, how much she would dare to tell the woman whom she knew so little and yet to whom she felt drawn as a friend she could trust. Polly, as well as being her daughter, was that, of course she was, but Polly was out of the country, and anyway ... She felt her mind slipping sideways. She'd think about it tomorrow, or rather, given the hour, later today. Drowning in sleep, slightly fuddled by the wine she had drunk, fatigued by the range of emotions she had been through, many of them new or anyway unfamiliar, she remembered her mother saying to her when she was a little girl, 'Tomorrow never comes, because when it's tomorrow it's today.' But it had of course come for her mother, that quick, brown fox. It came for everyone.

Her last waking thought was to wonder whether she would dream of foxes.

9

'WELL,' TRUDY SAID, RAISING HER GLASS of wine. 'Here's to you. And to Brighton. And to us. Any other, please specify, as James sometimes says.'

'Let's drink to friendship,' Julia said, as they clinked glasses. She met the other's gaze and, as she did so, felt a huge surge of relief. Waiting for Trudy's train to arrive she had been apprehensive, nervous even. Would the intense pleasure she had felt in the younger woman's company when they met in Greece survive transplantation to England? They had after all spent little more than a day together, and for all she knew, the Trudy Cosgrove of the island, with whom she felt such relaxed pleasure and who, despite the difference in their ages, seemed genuinely content, even gratified, to be with her, who opened-up, flower-like, in the warmth of Aegean sunlight, might prove to be a very different person in England.

But it was alright. This Trudy, who, waving, strode along the platform, who pushed her way boisterously through the ticket barrier and who kissed her on the cheek, saying as she did so, 'Hello, love, and thanks for getting me out of London for a day', – this Trudy was the one she remembered from a month earlier, the same eagerly smiling woman with whom she'd laughed over the pomposity of Giles Poynter and much else besides, and who, as they parted company under the flawless blue Greek sky, insisted they exchange telephone numbers, because 'We'll want to keep in touch, won't we', words she'd not offered as a hesitant question but as a confident assertion, so that Julia had been able to say 'Of course we will', feeling in the utterance what had to be gladness, a feeling that came to her again as she said to the woman now sitting opposite her, 'I'm so glad you could come.'

From the restaurant they looked out through plate-glass windows past the crowded promenade towards a stretch of sea glittering under the mid-day sun. 'Would you say this bears comparison with Greece?' she asked.

'Quite, quite different,' Trudy said. 'Here, we have the tide in all its English glory. We have a pier. We have a waiter who calls each of us "Madam". And,' she said pointing her fork at the plate of cheeses set before them, 'we also have Stilton. And Cheddar.'

Under a smart linen jacket she was wearing a dark-green open-neck blouse and well-cut jeans. A rope of chunky, white-painted wooden beads hung round her neck, enhancing a tan which had scarcely begun to fade.

'You look lovely,' Julia said, unenviously. She met the younger woman's clear-eyed gaze, her smile, the full-lipped mouth above a rounded, generous chin. 'James doesn't know how lucky he is.'

'Oh, James.' Trudy waved his name away with her raised fork. 'Now,' she said, pushing her plate aside, 'I want to know why you're here. Why Brighton?'

Lying behind the question was, Julia knew, the perfectly reasonable assumption that her telephone call two nights previously hadn't been simply to re-establish contact, and she, Trudy, who had after all detected and indeed commented on the fact that at one point in their telephone conversation Julia was crying, deserved an explanation as to why.

But it had been scarcely more than half an hour since she had met Trudy at the station, and Trudy had said, 'Let's walk down to the front, shall we? We could have some lunch and I know just the place to meet our needs.'

And as, arm-in-arm, they strolled along North Street and swerved into Ship Street, Julia told her new-found friend about how the previous day she'd taken a train to Chichester, wanting to see an exhibition at Pallant House and how she'd then gone into the Cathedral in order to visit the famous tomb. 'What tomb?' Trudy had asked, and Julia had said

'An Arundel Tomb' and Trudy had asked what was so famous about that, and why, if it was at Chichester, it was called the *Arundel* Tomb? – and Julia had laughed and briefly explained, and by the time she'd done that they'd arrived at their destination and, with Trudy leading the way, had entered the restaurant where Trudy chose a window table and ordered glasses of Sancerre for them both 'and a plate of your cheeses'.

And now the moment had come, and still she wasn't ready. 'Why Brighton?' she repeated, as though musing on the unexpectedness of Trudy's inevitable question. Then, speaking slowly as if she, herself, was less than certain as to why she was here, 'Because I decided I wanted to get away from home for a few days – before term starts – and I've never been to Brighton and it's supposed to be a lively place.'

The last words skidded off her lips, and Trudy laughed obligingly. 'I see. Brighton rocks,' she said. 'So it wasn't Orlando who lured you here? No romantic tryst.'

It was Julia's turn to laugh obligingly. 'I told you,' she said. 'Our meeting was a matter of pure chance. I hadn't even remembered he might be in Brighton. Besides, a fifty-year-old woman and a twenty-year-old man. I could get arrested for corrupting the morals of a juvenile.'

'He's twenty-two,' Trudy said, matter-of-factly.

Julia picked at a piece of bread. 'How do you know that?'

'James told me. After that scene on the beach between Orlando and his father, when we were on our own, James more or less exploded. He was angry, *really* angry with Orlando for embarrassing his friend in front of outsiders – me, I suppose he meant. Orlando ought to grow up, act his age. "Well out of order" is the phrase, isn't it?'

Julia wondered whether she should report to Trudy all that Orlando had said to her in the bar two nights earlier. Instead, 'Confession,' she said. 'I nearly lost my temper with Orlando the other evening.' And she gave Trudy a brief account of what had occurred between them. 'And all because he couldn't see the difference between two small words, "shut" and "closed". Ridiculous, I know. Still, teacher to dull student: I apologised to him for getting so heated about so trivial a matter.'

Trudy was looking at her closely. 'Obviously not trivial to you,' she said. Then, with seeming inconsequentiality, she asked, 'Julia, your phone. *Why* did you switch it off?'

'I told you,' Julia said, reaching for her glass. 'I didn't want people to know where I was.'

'But *why* didn't you want them to know? And what about your daughter? What about Martin? Suppose they tried to contact you, wouldn't they be worried that you weren't answering?'

'Polly's away in France with her partner. She won't phone before Sunday at the earliest, and I'll be back then.' But as she spoke the words she felt her heart lurch: with guilt, with resentment at the guilty feeling. *Why* should she feel accountable for her actions? Why couldn't she do as she damned well pleased?

Trudy said, 'Suppose something unforeseen happens to Polly? Sudden illness. An accident? It's been known.' The words came as a mild reproof, as though they had swapped roles and she was the older woman chastising a younger one for rash behaviour.

Julia turned to look across at people, ordinary people, holiday people, townspeople, moving to and fro along the promenade. After a few moments, pulse having slowed to what felt a more normal rate, she said, 'Albert – Al – her partner, has parents. He can contact them in an emergency.' Then, looking back at Trudy, she said, 'I'm not the only one who has to be needed.'

The puzzlement, bewilderment even, in Trudy's look, was now unmistakable. But all she said was, 'Accepting that you didn't want anyone to know where you were, I don't see why you couldn't have bought yourself a cheap phone here. You could have phoned your daughter – phoned Polly – even if you didn't want her phoning you.'

'I've only just enough cash to last me until Sunday.' Julia chose this time not to meet her friend's questioning gaze. 'I worked out what I'd need before I left. Strict budgeting.'

Then, she did lift her eyes and saw that her friend was shaking her head in mild exasperation. 'You presumably have a credit card?' Trudy asked.

'*No.*' Julia waited until she could control her breathing. 'No credit card. That would be traceable. And I don't want *that.*' She was, she knew, beginning to sound not merely unreasonable but quite possibly hysterical, close to tears. 'I really don't want ... ' But she broke off, asked, 'Does James always know where *you* are?'

'He knows I'm in Brighton,' Trudy said, 'and I know where *he* is.'

'So you made up your row.'

'We did.' Trudy picked up her glass and drained its contents in a single swallow. Holding it to her eye, she said, 'If you can believe what you see, you are looking at someone who has very recently accepted a proposal of marriage.' Then she returned the glass to the table and sat with both hands clasped round it.

'Oh, Trudy,' Julia said, reaching across to place her hand over her friend's, and squeezing. 'That's wonderful news.'

'Yes, well,' Trudy said, her lips twisted in a mock grimace. 'I told him he was a bit old for me, shop-soiled, and that he couldn't expect me to push him around in a wheelchair when he was a decrepit heap.' She tilted back her head and her laugh was loud enough to cause one or two nearby diners to look across at the pair of them. 'So that's the good news,' she said.

'And the bad news?' Julia asked, knowing it was expected of her.

'What have you got?' Trudy said. 'Yours is the bad news, isn't it?' She freed her hands from Julia's clasp and looked steadily into her eyes. 'Something's wrong, isn't it? Martin?' And when Julia stayed silent, Trudy said, 'He's in America. Presumably he'll want to be in touch, and yet you've come away and left your phone behind so he has no way of contacting you.'

'He *has* contacted me. He spoke to me as soon as he arrived. He told me he was well and that he'd seen Bay Bridge.'

'Fascinating,' Trudy said, 'Next thing you'll be telling me he's spotted a surfer.' Then, slapping her forehead, 'But no, silly me, I'm forgetting. He can't contact you. Not now.'

'He can leave a message.'

With a hint of exasperation, Trudy said, 'But meanwhile you don't want him to know where you are and you've taken good care that he can't trace you.'

'Nor can Polly,' Julia said faintly.

'This isn't about Polly, is it?' Trudy said, 'It's about Martin.'

Julia looked at her, then away. The restaurant where they sat seemed now to recede into a blur, its noises faded until she could hear nothing but the hammering of blood in her ears.

'Yes,' she said, 'alright. It's about Martin.' Then she lapsed into silence.

'Julia,' Trudy said, sighing, 'I don't want to seem rude. But the reason I'm in Brighton on a sunny day in late September is because, so you said on the phone the other night, you want to talk to me. If you've changed your mind, then fine, we can enjoy our day together and after that I'll return to London. But I don't think you have changed your mind, have you?' She looked keenly at Julia, then slowly nodded her head. 'OK. The floor, as they say, is yours. And whatever you want to talk about had better be a damned sight more important than a family spat or a common or garden quarrel with your husband. If it's either of those, I'll consider I've been lured here under false pretences. So, please, talk.'

'But not here,' Julia said. 'Can we first pay up and go?'

'Go where?'

'We could find a bench on the promenade.'

Trudy stood up decisively. 'Anything to oblige,' she said, adding 'And I'm hoping that when you've managed to tell me whatever it is that's bothering you we'll be able to enjoy the rest of the afternoon together. My train goes at five o'clock. Will that leave enough time?'

'I hope so,' Julia said.

10

THEY CHOSE A BENCH FACING THE SEA but far enough along the promenade for strollers and passers-by to be few in number. A scattering of sun-worshippers sprawled on the beach below where they sat, some lonely swimmers ploughed their way through the blue-green water, and one group of young men and women, thigh-deep among the incoming waves, their glistening bodies lithe with the sheer joy of flesh's uninhibited proximity, leapt to catch or bat away a beach-ball drifting erratically above them. All in the sexy airs of summer, Julia thought, and at that moment, remembering the sensual delight of pressing her own sea-damp flesh against Martin's as they lay on the sand after prolonged, leisurely immersion in the Aegean's yielding warmth, she gave an involuntary shudder.

Trudy glanced enquiringly at her.

'I was thinking,' Julia said, and the words came unbidden, 'of a story my mother told me, not long after she was widowed. A friend of hers, a long-time divorcee, was commiserating, and – my mother didn't know why, perhaps her friend thought it would help – this friend revealed that when her husband confessed his affair with a woman in the bank where they both worked and added that he wanted a divorce, she was completely taken aback. She'd suspected nothing. "And I thought I was happy," she told my mother.'

Julia paused, met Trudy's questioning gaze, and looked away, concentrating her own gaze on the frolickers in the surf. 'It was before my marriage,' she said. 'Mum said that she'd puzzled a good deal over her friend's words. How could the woman *not* have known? Or at least suspected.' Another pause. 'At the time I thought she was simply making conversation. But perhaps she was warning me.'

'I see,' Trudy said. She herself was now staring out to sea, shading her eyes with a hand as she watched one of the young men break away from the group in order to hurl himself into the air before twisting to dive back under the water's ruckled surface. 'Men were deceivers ever.'

'I read a poem when I was on the train coming down to Brighton,' Julia said. 'I don't remember every word of it but the poet, I think he must be a Roman poet, says reason proves that love deceives at every turn. "It hands back the ring, breaks every vow".'

Still shading her eyes, Trudy turned to Julia, a long, serious look. But she said nothing, waited for Julia to go on.

Julia said, 'But then the poet goes on to claim that nevertheless everyone's actions are compelled by love. "It's all we own". Do you think that's true?'

Trudy shrugged, pursed her lips. 'It doesn't leave much space for those who have to do without love,' she said.

'Perhaps they go mad,' Julia said.

Trudy put an arm round her. '*You're* not going to go mad, are you?' she said.

Julia pulled away, skewed her body round so she could look directly into Trudy's eyes. 'Why do you say that?' she asked.

'Because,' Trudy said, 'I'm assuming that what you really want to tell me is that your husband has left you. You've discovered that the whole American trip is a cock and bull story, a cover up so he can be off with his new woman.' Then, as Julia shook her head, 'Well, then, he's gone to America but he's taken a woman with him.'

'No, *that's* not it,' Julia said vehemently.

Trudy was bewildered. 'It's not? Then what is "it"?'

'I think I want to – ought to – leave Martin,' Julia said.

And then, speaking slowly and without pause, she explained why.

When she had finished – Trudy had let her talk, making no attempt to interrupt – her friend sat, shoulders slumped, elbows on knees, head between her hands, staring at a point in front of her elegant sandals.

After some minutes of silence between the two, Trudy straightened up and said, 'Let's go over some of this again, would you mind?' She glanced at her watch. 'We can carry on sitting here, or go for a walk, or take ourselves to a café. You choose.'

'Let's walk,' Julia said, 'I need to move.' And she stood.

Arm-in-arm the two women crossed from the promenade and began to walk slowly towards the Pavilion, from time to time standing aside to allow people who seemed in more haste than they themselves were to pass them, pausing at one point to watch a flurry of gulls squabble over the tipped-over refuse from a litter bin, but all the time talking, voices low as though they'd tacitly agreed on the need to keep their conversation to themselves.

When they reached their destination, Trudy looked at her watch and said, 'It's hardly worth going in, I'm afraid. My train leaves in not much more than half an hour.' She shrugged, 'Ah, well, it'll keep. Anyway', with a dismissive wave of the hand, 'I've been here, done that.'

'Oh, Trudy, I feel awful. I've ruined your day.'

Her words, spoken more loudly than she intended, were overheard by a couple about to enter the building who looked at them and then, eyebrows raised, at each other.

'Not at all,' Trudy said briskly. Then, in a measured way, she said 'Or if at all, in a good cause. It's what friendship's for, ducks.' And she gave Julia's arm a squeeze.

'Isn't it odd,' Julia said, as they turned away from the Pavilion. 'We know each other so little and yet we really do seem to be friends.'

'Sorority', Trudy said in mockney, 'is what I calls it.' And once more she squeezed Julia's arm.

At the ticket barrier they embraced and Julia said, 'You've helped me more than I can say. Perhaps ... I mean you won't ... ' And she paused, watching as Trudy searched in her bag for her ticket.

Trudy, several tickets now in hand, frowning in concentration as she selected the one she needed, said 'You're going to ask me not to mention any of this to James, aren't you? Don't worry.' Head now raised, 'I won't, promise. And you promise me to let me know as soon as you're home, and keep me informed, won't you, of what you plan?'

'I promise,' Julia said.

***

In her hotel room, lying propped up against her bed's headboard, wondering how to spend the evening, she thought back to her parting from Trudy and knew they would keep their promises to each other. Trudy the trustworthy. Odd, she thought, how friendships form. Slowly, most of them, but just occasionally friendship, like love, simply happens. It's the click of a lock as a box opens. But unlike love, the box won't slam suddenly, irrevocably shut, though because of altered circumstances and the passing of years it may slowly close. Shut. Close. There now, Orlando, that's the distinction.

She stood, went over to the small table where she'd left the book she'd brought with her to Brighton, found the poem she was looking for, and still standing read 'There's honesty, truth in what you do.' The honesty friends can share but which lovers can't, she thought. And as she went over to the window and looked out at the crowded street below as lights came on and cars and buses nosed their ways to different destinations, she found coming into her head yet again the scrawled message she had been carrying with her for the past days, the message – if that's what it was – she'd found tucked away in Martin's dictionary, those few poor words she had repeated to Trudy a few hours previously. *Martin, I can't go on. Tomorrow will be too late. Sandra.*

'Sandra?' Trudy had asked. 'Who's Sandra?'

'Sandra was a student of Martin's,' Julia told her. 'Years ago. Twelve years ago to be precise. Not long after he'd been made a professor.'

'Oh, dear.' Trudy had reached for Julia's hand. 'Poor Julia.' And then, after a moment of silence, 'You think that they had an affair?'

But then, as Julia said nothing, Trudy asked, her question urgent with dawning realisation, 'Or is this a more recent note? Has this Sandra turned up again? Is she making demands?'

'No, it's not that.' Julia shook her head. 'She can't do that. She's dead.' She watched her friend's expression turn from concern to bewilderment. 'Sandra died while she was still a student,' she said.

'About to take her finals, or she might already have taken them, I can't remember. I know it was in the summer.'

And then, wanting to tell Trudy all, and in some recess of her mind almost enjoying the dramatic effect of her words, she said, 'Sandra killed herself.'

11

WALKING AIMLESSLY ABOUT THE LANES OF Brighton on Saturday morning, Julia thought of all that Trudy had said by way of trying to reassure her, to persuade her that she, Julia, had very likely misinterpreted the meaning of the message she had chanced on. Sandra might have fantasised about Martin. The relationship was very likely all in the girl's mind. It had after all been known for women students, Trudy said drily, most of them away from home for the first time in their lives, to imagine themselves in love with one or other of their lecturers. As a newly arrived student at university herself, Trudy had, she told Julia, heard whispers about a finalist from the previous year, Yvonne Something-or-other, who had gone through a series of mad schemes to prolong her undergraduate career, convinced that if she could do so she would eventually make a lecturer, on whom she'd become fixated, return her love. The poor girl had at one point poured boiling water over her writing hand so that she couldn't sit her final exams. That way, she hoped, she could repeat the year, and it would give her enough time to make him come to his senses, so she was certain. But the head of the department, a wily old sod according to Trudy, had arranged for Yvonne to dictate her answers to one of the department's secretaries with shorthand skills.

'And I bet you can't guess what she did?' Trudy said. And without waiting for Julia to answer, she added, 'She bit off her tongue!'

'What, the *whole* of her tongue?' Julia was aghast.

'Enough to make it impossible for her to speak.'

'So what on earth happened?'

'According to what I heard her parents came and took her away. The rumour was that she'd been carted off to a psychiatric ward somewhere.'

Playing that story back in her head as she wandered the lanes, Julia accepted that the almost brutal flippancy of Trudy's anecdote had been an attempt to persuade her that the long-dead Sandra was in all likelihood a fantasist. Julia had been grateful to her friend, but she was unmoved. And she remained equally so when Trudy, having got her to reveal that she, Julia, presumably knew of Sandra's suicide because Martin had told her of it, said, 'Well, there you are, then. If he'd anything to hide he'd have kept schtum. Besides, *I can't go on. Tomorrow will be too late.* Honestly, it's so ... so, well, to be honest, it's the kind of thing you expect to come across in a Hollywood weepie. As if she was acting a part.'

Gazing out to sea, watching the young below as they sported on the beach, Julia said, 'They were her words, though, and she did kill herself.'

But Trudy was unpersuaded.

'Could be that she didn't mean to,' she said. 'Apparently far more women than men decide to commit suicide and then fail in the attempt. Either they swallow too few pills, or they make sure they'll be discovered before it's too late. Or,' she paused, then said, 'perhaps Sandra had cried wolf once too often.'

'Even so,' Julia told her, 'she must have been in a desperate way. And I knew nothing of that. *Nothing.*'

Now, as she mingled with the jostling, good-natured Saturday crowds, most of them making for the sea front, she thought, as so often she had since she'd come across Sandra's message, of herself and Martin, the two of them as they had been when young lovers. Not immediately in love, no, because at first they'd meant to be no more than friends, part of a larger group at university which included Giles and James, as well as others with whom they'd long lost touch, though Julia had for a while shared her bed with a student called Don Fletcher until Martin suddenly made it clear that he disapproved of Fletcher.

'He's a shit,' he told Julia, 'He's laughing at you behind your back, don't you know that?' – and Julia as suddenly discovered that, although she wasn't sure she believed Martin, she certainly didn't want to risk his disapproval, which had to mean that what they still referred to as a friendship was deepening, taking them further into themselves and each other. Deep enough to lead to their first clumsy, funny, sexual encounters, then into an ardency that came with their increasingly skilful love-making. Days as well as nights became taken up with the delights of discovering not merely each other's bodies but in what, as part of their private language, they called ordinary passions: hers for poetry and film, his for history and music, as well as shared pleasures, especially the up and downstream explorations in a hired rowing boat of the river that flowed past the university town whose buildings – churches, museum, magistrate's court housed in an old mansion, small art gallery, its walls for the most part lined with inconsiderable paintings by local not-so-contemporary artists – they also explored, although in spring and summer weather they preferred to ride out on borrowed bicycles into the surrounding countryside with its red-brick farms and small, one-street villages, each containing a pub where they could stop for glasses of habitually cloudy beer. Could there ever have been a time of such quality?

Trudy's voice broke in on her memories, the recall of her friend's questions dispelling her reverie. 'There was no suicide note? I mean nothing on the body? Nothing in the girl's room?'

'Not that I ever heard,' Julia had told her. 'Not according to the police, either. There was no note. That's what we all believed. That's what *I* believed, until I found the one hidden in Martin's study.'

'But why would Martin hold onto a note that might, so you seem to be suggesting, implicate him in the girl's death?'

Julia was now passing the café where Orlando worked, but she walked steadily on. She had no desire to see him again. But, recalling their evening in the bar, the image of the elderly man who had sought out her company came back to her, his tale of loneliness, of the dead wife, dispersed family, and shaking her head she forced herself to concentrate on the group of students, as they surely were, who spread across the lane ahead of her as they sauntered in the direction of the pier.

But then she remembered the look in her friend's eyes, one of contrite acknowledgement, as she said to Trudy, 'That's not the question. The question is why should he hide it?'

And then came the memory of how, inevitably, and after a considered pause, Trudy had asked the obvious question, 'Why not ask him?'

'Because,' Julia said, 'In the first place he's on the other side of the world.'

Trudy had turned to her, and her eyes were now challenging her. 'And in the second place?' she had asked.

'Sandra was pregnant.'

* * *

Saturday afternoon was spent in wandering through the Pavilion's many rooms, trying to look at paintings and furnishings of which, afterwards, she retained no clear memories. That evening, fitting her few belongings into the travel bag she had brought to Brighton, thinking as she did so of the unruffled companionship in which so recently she and her husband, about to leave the island, had completed their packing, she sat on the side of her bed and, about to give way to tears, shouted at herself, 'Stop it, *stop it.*'

Once again she opened the book she had brought with her – it was lying open on her bedside table – and ran her eyes over the poem that had taken possession of her. 'We'll stay home, light fires, drink wine and put the times to right/In song.'

She shut the book and threw it into her bag.

Then she got to her feet, stood, fists clenched.

'Fuck you, Martin,' she said aloud.

III

12

SUNDAY MORNING, JULIA WAS OUT OF bed early, and after showering, dressing, packing, and pulling wide the curtains on another blue day, went down to breakfast taking her bag with her.

The dining room was empty, although she noticed a youth in open-necked white shirt and dark jeans propped against the kitchen door and watching with mild curiosity as she looked around at the unlaid tables.

'Is it possible for me to have breakfast?' she asked him.

He shook his head. 'Nothing doing before nine o'clock,' he said. 'Not on Sundays. Anyway, the cook's not here. Probably got ratted last night.'

Julia glanced at her watch. 'It's very nearly nine,' she said. 'Perhaps you could manage to make me a cup of coffee and some toast.'

He looked dubious. 'Dunno about the toast,' he said, 'but coffee, yeah, OK. Instant do you?'

She pointed to a sign pinned to the wall beside the door where he lounged. 'That says freshly-brewed coffee is always available.'

'Not now it ain't, no chance. Not without the cook.'

'Can I speak to the manager?'

He shook his head. 'He's in Amsterdam. Won't be back until tonight.'

'Then who's in charge?'

'In charge? No idea, not me for one.'

Julia picked up her bag. 'Thank you for your help,' she said, walking away.

'You're welcome,' he called after her.

A brisk fifteen-minute walk brought her to the station, and by mid-morning she was on a train out of St Pancras, heading for Leicester. She had bought a Sunday newspaper to read on the journey but spent most of the time looking out at the early autumn landscape, the still lush fields and small red-brick towns lazing in unbroken sunlight, the canal, without boats or barges, that accompanied her curving journey for much of the way through the Midlands, the ribbon of water gleaming intermittently beyond thick hedgerows and an occasional clump of trees, almost, she thought, like a half-forgotten secret, once precious, now all but lost to memory.

But as she came closer to her destination, her mood changed from melancholy resignation to anger, to resolve. The bus journey from station to the top of her road was a mere twenty minutes but she wanted to get indoors. She had a phone call to make.

Walking up the path to her front door, she saw that a piece of paper was poking from her letter-box. She pulled it free, unlocked the door, stooped to pick up the few letters that lay on the doormat, and only when, having dropped her travel bag at the foot of the stairs, and gone into the kitchen, did she unfold the paper.

At which moment, there was a rapping on the front door.

Her next-door neighbour stood in the porch, shears in hand.

'I see you got my note,' she said, pointing to the paper Julia was holding.

'I've not had time to read it,' Julia said, 'I've only this moment got in.' She opened the door wider, in mute invitation.

Her neighbour stood silent.

'I'm about to make myself a cup of tea,' Julia said, and feeling she owed the woman an explanation, or perhaps apology, though for what she couldn't say, added, 'Can I offer you one, Muriel?'

Her use of the name, hesitant though it was, did the trick.

Propping her shears against the porch lintel, Muriel Dawson stepped past Julia into the hall, glancing as she did at the travel bag before she made her way along the hall to the kitchen.

'I've been away for a few days,' Julia said, motioning her guest to a seat. 'Let me put the kettle on and then I'll read your note.'

'It's about your daughter, your Polly.'

'*Polly?* Why ... what ... She's alright, isn't she?'

Accident? Injury? Illness? ... What had happened to Polly? Panic constricted her throat. Whatever could have convinced her to keep her movements secret from her daughter?

'No need to worry,' her guest said. 'She phoned me because she couldn't get through to you. She was worried about *you*.'

Julia drew breath, her heart still hammering. 'When was this?'

'Last night. She said she'd tried you several times but your mobile was turned off and you weren't answering on your landline.'

'Because I wasn't here.'

Muriel, her look one of reproof, said, 'But Polly didn't know that.' Lips pursed, she added, 'And nor did I, of course.' Though I ought to have been told, her look said.

Julia dropped tea bags into two mugs, poured boiling water over them, stirred the bags round, hoiked them out and set them on the draining board as she asked 'Milk? Sugar?'

'Just the usual,' her guest said, her words implying that Julia ought to remember how she took her tea, though she'd been so rarely in Julia's house that no, Julia did *not* remember.

But she fetched milk from the fridge, placed it on the table between them, and watched the other woman splash a very little into her full cup. 'I'll know next time,' she said.

Muriel took a sip of tea then, placing her mug back on the table, said, 'Of course, not knowing where you were, I couldn't tell Polly. But I said I'd come round, see if anything was the matter, and phone her back. So I did, banged on the door, walked round the house and peered in the downstairs windows, but couldn't see anything. I was wondering whether to call the police, but when I spoke to Polly again – goodness knows how much *that* will have cost me – she said not to worry, she'd try again today.'

'I'll phone her now,' Julia said, looking at the kitchen clock. 'And I'm sorry about the expense you've been put to. I'll pay for the cost of the call, of course I will.'

'Oh, no need,' the neighbour said, exuding sudden largesse. 'As long as you're well, that's the important thing.'

She swallowed the rest of her tea, and stood. 'We all need a break now and then.' Her desire to know where Julia had been, what she'd been up to, was so blatant, that Julia decided to tell her.

'I went to Brighton' she said.

'Brighton?' Muriel's look, the widened eyes, the way she pronounced the word, suggested near disbelief.

'A few days of relaxation before teaching begins.' Julia was edging the other woman out of the kitchen and towards the front door, making light of her revelation.

As she stood on the porch, Muriel, retrieving her shears, asked, 'How is Professor Gibbs? All well?'

'As far as I know,' Julia said, smiling.

Her neighbour nodded. 'These men,' she said, 'they never give much away, do they? I had to drag everything out of David.' And when it was plain that Julia would say no more, she added, 'Well, I'm pleased you're back, safe and sound. And thanks for the cuppa.'

Julia watched until Muriel had closed the front gate behind her then hurried back into the kitchen. She must speak to Polly.

And she must also phone San Francisco. I had to drag everything out of David. Well, she, Julia, was all set to drag the truth from Martin. Running again through the questions – the demands – she had rehearsed on the train from St Pancras, she lifted the receiver. She'd get him tell her the truth about Sandra ... Sandra – *Hutchinson.* Yes, Sandra Hutchinson. Right then.

She switched on her mobile and found she had six text messages.

Two were from Polly. *Hi, Mum.This is Wednesday. We're having a great time. See Vezeley and die. Tomorrow we'll be in Aix. Love you, Polly.* Then, two days later, *Hi Mum. Friday. Your mobile's switched off. Dad says he's tried you a few times but no answer. Call him will you if you get this message? He's worried. Al sends love and love from me. P*

Julia deleted both messages and then texted Polly. *Have been away for a few days. I'm a free woman after all! Back now, Sunday, and geared up for college. Look forward to hearing details of your grand tour. Much love – and to Al – Mum.*

The other messages were all from Martin. She felt wrong-footed. No doubt he'd be rebuking her for having switched off her mobile. Why should she apologise to *him*? I'll deal with them, deal with *him*, once I've made myself a sandwich, she thought, then, realising that in her haste to get away she'd made no provision for her return and that she had no food in the house, swore silently, reached for a shopping bag. There was still time to get to the local supermarket before it closed.

Half an hour later she was back at the house, unpacking a small sliced loaf, a block of Cheddar, a carton of eggs, and a bunch of bananas, enough to see her through the rest of the day. I'll shop properly tomorrow, she thought, as she stowed her purchases, and, before closing the fridge door, reaching for a half-full bottle of Sauvignon.

Sitting at the table, full glass at her elbow, she reached for the mobile. Now for Martin. Keying in the numbers, she remembered the last line of a poem she had read in her student days. *And this is going to be how history starts*, she quoted to herself.

13

BUT OF COURSE IT WASN'T. IN the first place she had stupidly not bothered to check the time difference between England and the American West Coast. When Martin finally answered the phone his voice was groggy with sleep. In the second, Julia found that without being able to see him, to *actually* confront him, she was at a loss for words. If she couldn't *see* his reaction, how could she ask him, no, tell him, that now, after all these years, she had discovered about his affair with that student, that Sandra Hutchinson, had found about it by accident?

'By accident?' She could hear his voice, the note of scornful disbelief, and, then, when she told him how she came upon the scrap of paper, his outraged response. 'Prying, snooping. Destroying the trust between us. And then misunderstanding the meaning of those few words into the bargain.'

Suppose he said that, any of it, what was she to answer?

Besides, suppose she *had* misunderstood? Distance destroyed intimacy. It also wiped away the possibility of candour. If she could have looked into his eyes she'd have known whether he was telling the truth. But she couldn't. Instead, she heard herself apologising for waking him from sleep. 'What time is it where you are? Not yet seven o'clock. Oh, god, Martin. I'm sorry.' *She* was apologising to *him*.

'You're welcome.' A brief laugh. 'See, I'm learning to speak the local lingo.'

His yawn was audible. But his next words stunned her. 'By the way, what took you to Brighton? We don't know anyone there, do we?'

It was a moment before she could reply with a question of her own. 'How did you find out about Brighton?' It sounded, she realised, like an admission of guilt.

Over the phone his voice, muffled by yet another yawn, Martin said, 'Giles told me, last evening – West Coast time.' A pause to let the implied rebuke make its mark. Then, 'He got the info from Orlando.' A further pause, before, with what might have been studied casualness, but how could she tell, he added, 'According to Giles you and Orlando spent an evening drinking together in some sleazy den.' His laugh, a way of making light of the matter, also contained, she sensed, an invitation for her to explain herself. He had wrong-footed her without even knowing the accusation she had been wanting him to answer.

Forced into awkward laughter, 'I think I've become a sea and sun junkie,' she said. 'I fancied a few more days of both before the start of teaching, that's all.'

No, it wasn't all, far from it, but the conversation had by now veered so wildly from the one she'd mapped out that she had no option but to explain about the chance meeting with Orlando which had led to their decorous evening of drink and casual conversation.

'I see.'

'I hope you do. And now,' she concluded, 'you can tell me why Giles was phoning you. Surely not just to let you know that I'd bumped into his son and we'd had a drink together.' Though it wasn't beyond Giles, she knew, to enjoy the chance of putting one over on Martin.

'He wanted to know whether I'd been able to arrange for him to give a guest lecture here.'

'God, there's no stopping him, is there? What did you say?'

'That I'd asked around but the omens weren't good.'

'And had you? Asked around?'

'Giles is an old friend.'

Julia drank some wine. 'If it had been me I'd have told him to ... what do Americans say? ... take a hike.'

'No, you wouldn't,' Martin said.

Which, she thought ruefully when after a few minutes more she put the phone down, was probably true. She sat looking at the receiver, numbed by her own – what was it? – cowardice, refusal to tell Martin that she knew about him and Sandra. Anyone listening in to their conversation would have taken it to be an entirely mundane exchange between man and wife. It had even ended with his telling her he loved her, and though she hadn't responded to that neither did she use any of the words she'd been hoarding for the past week, sharpening them each time she took them out for inspection, honing them for the job of cutting him out of her life for once and for all.

* * *

She admitted this to Trudy when, some hours later, having made and eaten a cheese sandwich, and decided against another glass of wine, she phoned her friend.

She began, though, by telling Trudy about Giles's attempt to get himself invited to San Francisco, adding that Orlando had told his father about bumping into her in Brighton. 'So of course Giles passed the news onto Martin. Typical Giles,' she said.

'What is?' Trudy asked, 'Hoping for Martin to do him a favour? There'd be no reason, would there, not to mention Orlando's bumping into you. Or was it the other way round?' The voice coming down the phone sounded unusually abrupt, and Julia realised that Trudy was probably hoping for an uninterrupted day with James.

Apologetically, she said, 'No, I suppose not. But flying across the world to give a lecture? That's a bit much, isn't it? And I'd be surprised, wouldn't you, if his university allowed him the time off at such short notice. Unless,' the thought came with the force of revelation, 'unless he'd got the whole thing planned. All he needed was an invitation.'

Trudy said, 'He'd have no difficulties getting away. The university would be right behind him. Think of the kudos. Think of the headline! PROFESSOR INVITED TO LECTURE AT PRESTIGIOUS AMERICAN INSTITUTION. Besides, he could be there and back in three days. James does it all the time. He's more often in the air than on the ground. Now you see him, now you don't. But right now, I'm seeing him. He's sitting across from me at the table, tongue out, waiting for his dinner.'

Abashed, Julia said, 'Oh, Trudy, I'm sorry. I'll get off the phone. And you're right. Space shrinks all the time.' But as she said the words she thought of the distance between herself and Martin and how, in the absence of proximity, she had found herself in trivial conversation with the man she had intended to repudiate. 'I couldn't tell him, I *couldn't*,' she said.

Clearly wanting to end the call, Trudy said matter-of-factly, 'Probably better to keep it that way till he's back.'

'I don't want him back,' Julia said, and put the phone down.

She sat at the table, miserable, baffled, poured herself the glass of wine she'd previously rejected, and only then remembered she must phone Polly. What's the matter with me? she thought. I'm going to pieces. But as she waited for Polly to speak she told herself not to be a self-pitying wimp. And when the answerphone informed her that nobody was there to answer and to leave a message so that 'we can get back to you', she was able to speak calmly, explain that she had been away for a few days but was now home, and had reassured Muriel that all was well. 'So no need to answer this,' she ended, 'but I'll expect a full account of your holiday when you and Al are back home.'

Then, ending the call, she reached for her still full glass and took it upstairs with her, chose what she would wear for tomorrow's meeting at college, stripped, showered, found herself hoping despite her own words that Polly would get in touch, admitted as she got into bed that her putting the phone down so abruptly on Trudy would require an apology, feared it might have damaged their burgeoning friendship, turned on her pillow, looked across the expanse of empty bed to where the last glimmerings of evening light haunted the window whose curtains she hadn't bothered to draw, and thought, this is no good, this self-induced misery, *ecrasez l'infame*, and, as she drifted into sleep, tried without success to remember where the words came from.

* * *

'So,' Janine Hamilton said, 'now we're all here I suggest we begin.' She smiled graciously at Julia who took her seat with an apologetic bow to the chair – 'I'm so sorry, there was a road accident, the bus was delayed' – and held up her agenda paper. 'Before we run through the items here, I'd like to introduce our new full-time member of staff, Dr Anthony Rayburn. That's Rayburn with a *y* rather than the *e* of the great Scottish artist.' Her smile, which included them all, was meant as a reminder, not that they needed it, that she herself was Scottish, or as she sometimes said, a daughter of the Ancient Kingdom of Fife. 'Dr Rayburn – Anthony – will be replacing our recently retired colleague Jim Wilson as Head of History. Perhaps it will help him if we go round the table introducing ourselves and our subject areas. I'll begin, shall I? Mrs Janine Hamilton, Principal and, whenever I can be spared from administrative chores, ready to put my shoulder to the wheel – or should that be reel – of Media Studies.'

After the obligatory titter, the others, including several part-timers, Julia among them, identified themselves.

'Though I guess you don't remember many of our names,' Graham Richards, who taught Art said, as, meeting over, a group of them sat round a table in a nearby pub.

'This is where the real meetings happen,' someone else advised the new man. 'The Royal Oak is where we come to plot and counterplot. Free from Authority and its spies. Unless, that is, walls have ears.' He looked with mock-suspicion round the room they were in, leant forward, and lowering his voice to a conspiratorial whisper, said, 'I'm Andrew Jenkins, Andy to all and sundry. What do you like to be called, can I ask? Dr Rayburn? Anthony? Tony?'

'Tony will be fine.'

Julia said, smiling, 'Take no notice of Andy's way of behaving. He whispers because he's naturally paranoid. If Janine so much as sneezes he suspects it's a warning that we're all going to be fired.' And when the new man laughed, she said, 'It was probably the same at your former place of work.'

He smiled, playing along, said 'We were *all* paranoid at our college.'

'And where was that?' Graham Richards asked. 'We're keen to know.'

'Manchester,' he said. And in answer to a further question that came from the Media Studies woman to his left, dramatic in black leggings and black, wool sweater, 'I was a student at Reading.'

'Reading? Well, well,' Julia said. Then, when he looked enquiringly at her, she asked, 'I don't suppose you knew a lecturer there called Giles Poynter?' As she spoke she took in Rayburn's grey jacket, blue-check shirt, black cords, and thought, academic uniform, the same the world over, or anyway, England.

'Giles Poynter? Professor Poynter? He was Head of the Department. Do you – did *you* know him?'

'We were students together.'

Leaning across the table, Graham Richards said, 'Julia's husband is the famous Martin Gibbs. A star in the academic firmament.'

But any spark of satiric intent in his words was doused by Rayburn's response. 'Wow,' he said, 'Martin Gibbs, eh? Yes, he's a big name.' He let his gaze wander round the table and said, 'I remember Poynter invited him to give a guest lecture. One of the great moments of my not very great undergraduate career.' He was looking at Julia with new respect. 'I've read all his books. I'd love to meet him sometime.'

Julia finished the orange juice which was all she'd permitted herself, and stood up. 'He's in America for a month. San Francisco,' she said. But aware that it would have been ungracious to have left matters at that point, as though she was meaning to slam the door on his implied request, she said to Rayburn, 'I hope you'll be happy here. Nice to have met you. No, don't bother to get up.'

But he did, and as he took her hand, and she registered the firmness of his grip and what seemed a genuine enough smile, he said, 'It's a privilege to meet you, Mrs Gibbs.'

Which, she thought, as she waited for her bus, translates into, It's a privilege to meet the wife of the great Professor Martin Gibbs, satellite to his sun, palely reflecting some of his glory as she orbits his universe. And as she walked towards her house, irritation turned to a smouldering anger. A part-time teacher of no consequence, not worth more than a glance until she's known to share Martin Gibbs's bed, that's me.

Some minutes later, standing in her kitchen and wondering what to prepare for supper, whether, indeed, she could be bothered to eat, she said aloud, 'Well, Dr Rayburn, what will you have to say when you find that I no longer share that bed. That I, Julia Gibbs, am me, myself, alone.'

14

JULIA WROTE:

Tuesday evening. I bought this notebook on the way home from college. Having suggested to my classes that they should keep journals in order to help their efforts to write and think clearly, I thought, well, Ms Gibbs, why not practise what you preach? I probably won't find the time to maintain it on a day-to-day basis, but having it to refer to and to confide in will, I think, be something of a comfort. And if that turns out to be a mistaken assumption, I'll simply stop keeping it. At this moment, though, I feel quite excited. Why, I might even find that it's becoming like one of those intimate confessionals I used to enjoy reading in nineteenth-century novels: the Brontes, Dickens, Wilkie Collins – Collins above all. (M as Fosco.) Damn. Cut *that* out. Reader over my shoulder, shove off. *I* know why I'm writing, and it isn't to entertain you. But if you're still there you might as well know that the reason I may want to spend some time each evening on this journal is quite simply that I'm lonely. Not something I can tell anyone else, but it's the fact. Why? Why am I lonely? Well, obviously, because I'm on my own. Yes, I've been on my own before. After all, the great Professor is often invited here, there, and everywhere to lecture, and sometimes he's been away for weeks, or even more, at a time. But *afterwards* he's come back, returned to our house as a matter of course. 'I thought we were happy.' Ha! Now, though, I don't want him back, words I repeated to Trudy when I wrote yesterday to apologise for ending Sunday's telephone conversation so abruptly. (Which reminds me. When I bumped into Graham Richards early this morning he congratulated me on being on time for classes. 'No traffic hold-ups today?' He's fly, old Graham. He knew that my excuse for arriving late at the staff meeting was pure invention. What he *didn't* know was how many drafts of the letter to Trudy I'd torn up. I couldn't afford to get the tone of that wrong. Whatever I

97

do, I don't want to lose her friendship.) [*Break*]

That was a phone call from Polly. Such joy to hear her voice, even when she was rebuking me for going off without warning. And Brighton! Why Brighton? Because, I said, I'd never been there, which seemed to satisfy her, but I wonder whether she noticed my silence when she told me M had been in contact and told her that he'd spoken to me. Was he fishing? But that would mean he was suspicious of ... of what? Not me and Orlando, surely! And he surely doesn't know that I found Sandra's note? Polly told me that she and Al are now in Brittany and loving their time together in France. Did I receive her card from Aix? Yes, thanks, I did. Good! And they'll be home on Saturday. Very good!! And how was work? Was I pleased to be back teaching? To make her laugh – not that *her* spirits needed to be raised – I told her about the ridiculous mess I got into with a class today. A youth questioned the title of the Hardy poem I'd asked them to consider. 'Paying Calls'. But who *was* Calls, he wanted to know, and why should he be paid? Was he Hardy's landlord? And why wasn't his name mentioned in the poem? I tried to explain that Hardy was paying a visit to dead friends, like someone dropping in for a chat. 'Talking to dead friends?' he asked. 'Why?' 'Because he's a nutter,' someone called out. Laughter all round. Laughter from Polly, too. I didn't tell her the rest. Anyway she wanted to let me know that she and Al would try to get to Leicester in a couple of weeks' time, 'when Dad's back.' Oh, god. What am I going to tell her? *When* am I going to tell her?

She closed the notebook, stretched, then, with a buoyancy she certainly hadn't felt when an hour earlier she sat down and uncapped her pen, and which for now at least was scarcely lessened by the fraught questions on which she'd ended her first entry, she sprang up and, light on her toes, crossed to the fridge. Sipping the glass of wine she had awarded herself, she realised with a kind of elation that the very act of writing was more than a way of filling spare time. It was a form of absorption. She wished now that she'd told Polly more about the poetry class she'd taught that afternoon. It might have prompted her to make it part of her journal entry, to join the comic misunderstanding about the title of Hardy's poem. For all she knew, that had been a diversionary tactic from serious business by the lad who had seemingly appointed himself class clown and who enjoyed 'flummoxing' his tutor. A good word, flummoxing, one her mother had often used. Well, if Ryan Simmons or whatever his name was had meant to flummox her she bore him no ill will. If anything, he had helped settle the others to the task of talking about Hardy's poem.

But there had been another moment which, more than flummoxing her, would, to use another of her mother's expressions, have tried the patience of a saint. A solemn owl of a student, one among an increasing number of foreign teenagers the college enrolled, wanted to know what, as Hardy's poem turned out not to be concerned with debt repayment, it *was* about. 'Please to tell us what is the answer.'

With a degree of assurance she later understood the young man wouldn't have appreciated, Julia trotted out the obvious response to his appeal. 'A poem isn't like the solution to a scientific problem. There is no *final* answer.' And when he frowned – in disagreement, uncertainty, plain dissatisfaction? – she added, 'It's important for you to consider the poem from your own perspective.' The frown deepened. 'I mean your *personal* response is what matters. Though of course that will probably be influenced by our discussion.'

He said, 'But I wish to gain good marks in my examination. I wish you to tell me what I should think.' He didn't say, 'That's what you're paid for,' but she knew he must be thinking it. At the staff meeting Andy Jenkins had raised the matter of the influx of foreign students. 'They'll soon be strangling the life out of the home-grown variety.' Seeing the nods, Janine Hamilton had said, with more than a hint of weary petulance, 'Andy, you know as well as I do that we need them.' She looked round the table. 'They stand between you and job losses, *that's* why we welcome them. We need them as much as they need us. And as you also know, some of them are damned good, and most of them work harder than the native variety.'

Recalling the Principal's words as she picked at slices of cheddar she'd cut from a large wedge, Julia thought, and if there *are* to be losses, it's part-timers who'll be heaved overboard first. And she was jolted into embarrassment, even shame, by the memory of her glib words to Duncan Chan – was that his name? He had looked first sceptical, then dismissive. She didn't blame him.

But she enjoyed her week's teaching. The students, fresh to the work, were, most of them, alert to her promptings; and a surprisingly large number of the fifteen who had enrolled for Literature were keen to take part in class discussion. When she reported this on Friday lunchtime as she sat with others in the staff room unwrapping her sandwiches, Andy Jenkins stared sceptically at her. 'Like stirring mud at the bottom of a pond, with my lot,' he said. 'Seeing if I could detect any signs of life.'

Graham Richards grimaced in mock despair. 'Why don't we ask the new boy how it's been for him?' he said, turning to greet Tony Rayburn who, as he came to sit with them, reached in his bag for a thermos and, then, an apple. 'No complaints so far,' Rayburn said. He bit into the apple, chewed, used a thumbnail to pick at a shred of apple-skin that had snagged between what Julia noticed were white, full teeth, and studying the obstruction on the end of his nail, said reflectively, 'I've only one lad, though, among fourteen lasses.'

'Lucky him,' Jenkins said.

'He seems a bit cowed.'

'Well, then,' Graham Richards said, 'lucky you', and held his hands up in a form of apology. 'I mean with those odds you often find the one male determined to argue the toss with the old bloke in charge. Prove who's cock of the walk.'

Julia, glancing at Rayburn's unperturbed expression, thought 'He'll have no problem seeing off the opposition.'

***

It was a thought that recurred to her as, later that afternoon, she joined him and other members of staff in the Principal's office, for what Janine called 'Sherry and Debriefing'. Once term settled in and evening classes began in earnest, there would be no chance for other than official meetings, so Janine always used these occasions at the beginning of a teaching year to, so she said, lend an ear to teething problems. The upshot was that they stood around in awkward silence while she dispensed sherry – one glass each was the understood allowance – and made stiff enquiries about how they thought term would shape up.

Among the gathering, Julia noticed, Tony Rayburn seemed most at his ease. He found replies, neither condescending nor effusive, to the various inanities offered him by those who could think of anything to say, and when Janine, pausing in her relentless progress round the room, asked him rather too loudly, 'And what do you make of us so far?' he said, smiling broadly, 'So far so good. I'll come back to you if and when anything changes.'

The words, his smile, courteous though both were, seemed to unsettle Janine. Colouring a little, she said 'Please do', and passed abruptly on.

***

Some half an hour later, as Rayburn walked with Julia away from college, he said, 'You looked back there as though you were enjoying yourself as much as I was.'

'And how much was that?'

'Not at all.'

Laughing, Julia said, 'I hadn't realised I'd made it so obvious.' Then, as they stood at the side of the road that would take her to her bus-stop, she said, 'Those are always starchy occasions, I'm afraid. I don't think anyone enjoys them, but we all have to pretend. It's Janine's way of implying that the college is a place of grace and favour, several cuts above the FE grade.'

She was about to say farewell and leave him, but 'Fancy a quick drink?' he asked her. He hunched up his shoulders, shuddered extravagantly. 'I could do with getting rid of the taste of that sherry.'

'I know the very place,' Julia said, and a few minutes later they were sitting at a table in a wine bar before filled glasses which, despite his protests, she'd insisted on paying for, red for him, her customary white, and he was asking her about Janine. 'That suit she was wearing. Expensive material, I'd guess, and, also at a guess, made to measure.'

Janine's dark blue trouser suit was, Julia knew, no off-the-peg bargain, not like the grey skirt and favourite maroon sweater she herself was wearing. 'If you're thinking a principal's salary won't run to such couture, you should see her house – mansion, rather. But then her husband's a solicitor.'

'And they dine off gold plates.'

She laughed, said, raising her voice above the sudden blast of wall-music, 'I wouldn't know, I've never been invited. None of us has, not as far as I know.'

Instead of replying, Rayburn stood and walked across to the bar. By the time he was back the music had been turned down to a bearable level.

'Now we can hear each other speak,' he said, dropping into his seat. And he told her of an occasion in Manchester when he and a colleague had visited a tapas bar where the music was so loud they'd had to shout their orders at the young woman who came to attend to them. 'Couldn't you turn the music down?' Rayburn's colleague had asked her. 'We want to talk.' She'd looked mystified. 'Talk?' she asked. 'What for? This is a restaurant.' Registering Julia's cocked eyebrow, Rayburn said, 'It's true. Those were her very words.'

Julia said, 'I believe you.' The bar they were in was beginning to fill, men and women in business suits, work finished for the week, an almost electric thrill of expectancy in the air, that Friday evening feeling, a whole weekend ahead, a lifting of spirits she remembered from her own student days and one that lingered for some years afterward. But not now, not now. 'Years ago the place to meet for food and talk was any Indian restaurant,' she said. 'Then pizza parlours began to muscle in. And now I suppose tapas bars are all the rage.'

Rayburn nodded. 'Though the choice is wide,' he said. 'Even when I was a student there seemed to be a new restaurant opening every week.'

It was Julia's turn to agree. 'I remember my mother telling me that when she was young eating out was a luxury. "Once in a blue moon was all your Dad and I could afford," she told me. "Now you young folk think nothing of going to a restaurant." And that,' Julia said, 'was thirty years ago.' She tried to laugh off the sudden feeling of self-consciousness. 'When you were still in short trousers.'

Rayburn said, seriously, 'I was at Uni fifteen years ago.'

'By which time my husband was a professor – just.'

He drained his glass. 'And I heard him lecture in my second year. Bloody good it was, too. A sight more enlivening than anything served up by ... ' He stopped, blushed faintly, no doubt remembering that she was friendly with Giles Poynter. As though to cover the awkward moment he had caused, he raised his glass, looked enquiringly at her. 'Fancy another?'

'No.' Julia stood, smiled. 'No thanks. I need to get back.'

Rayburn too stood. 'You're probably right,' he said. He picked up his bag. 'I'll buy next time.'

As they stood outside, in the early evening cool, he added, 'Better not let the wine get to my head.' Then, by way of explanation, 'I need the weekend for study.'

'Oh?'

'Something I'm working on.'

Julia waited until a couple had brushed past them on their way into the wine bar before she said, mockingly, 'It sounds awfully hush-hush as they used to say in spy novels.'

Rayburn laughed. 'Nothing that exciting, I'm afraid.' He held out his hand. 'Enjoy your weekend, Mrs Gibbs.'

As she took it she spoke the words she knew were expected of her. 'Call me Julia,' she said.

15

BACK HOME SHE SWITCHED ON HER phone and found she had two text messages. One, from Martin, read *Yr machine off again. Back in Brighton perhaps? Ha, Ha. Hot here. Hot there? x M.* Wondering for the first time if he was, perhaps, nonplussed, even made suspicious by her apparent non-communicability, her heart gave a little skip. Guilt? Pleasure? Guilty pleasure, perhaps. *Staff get-together*, she texted back. *Janine forbids machines while she's in saddle. Keep cool.* She herself scarcely understood what the words meant, though it was true that the Principal did frown on the use of personal phones during what she called office hours. It apparently set bad habits, encouraged, so she said, students to think it permissible to contact 'all and sundry'. Still, *Keep cool*? She cancelled those words then pressed the send button.

The other message was from Polly. *Hi, Mum. In Rostock and about to board car ferry. Will speak tomorrow. Love P and A.* Replying to that was easy. *Safe journey. Look forward to hearing abt yr hols. Love to you both, M.*

Preparing a salad while she listened to a favourite CD, Finzi's settings of poems by Hardy – *Earth and Air and Rain* it was called – she sang under her breath in accompaniment to the baritone's 'And we shall see the waters spring/Waters spring/From chinks the scrubby copses crown ... /"We shall" I say: but who may sing/Of what another moon will bring."' And as she sang, she began for the first time in what seemed like ages, though in fact it was a mere two weeks, to feel an uncomplicated happiness seeping through chinks in her consciousness, a happiness which, for the moment at least, reversed Hardy's habitual apprehensive caution of 'what another spring may bring'. For Hardy, she was all-too aware, tomorrows were usually harbingers of suffering or loss. But tomorrow, Saturday, Julia's loved daughter would be home.

Later, as she washed her glass and plate, she wondered whether she should tell Polly about an amusing incident involving one of her students that day, but no, she thought, I can't expect Polly to take an interest in classroom babble, her world is so different from mine. And as she thought that, the happiness of a few minutes earlier began to seep away. How little she really knew of Polly's life in London. And how little she could tell her daughter of her own.

In particular, what was she to say when Polly asked, as she was sure to do, about her father. 'Have you heard from Dad? Did he tell you how anxious he was when he couldn't make contact?' What, for that matter, had Polly said to him about her mother's strange decision, as it must seem, to spend those days in Brighton? That would, Julia acknowledged as she searched for clingfilm in which to wrap the remains of the salad, have in some way to be explained to Polly, and then she herself would probably discover that father and daughter had puzzled over it jointly, had even come to a shared agreement that – that what? That Julia had acted in a manner which neither could relate to the wife and mother they knew, and what could explain *that*? His rock of dependability, Martin had sometimes called her, and though she had bridled at the phrase when he first used it – it made her sound, she protested, an insensate lump – she was secretly pleased to be thought of as the person he, and for that matter Polly, regarded as the still point in their turning worlds.

And then, without telling either, she had gone to Brighton.

To try to explain her behaviour to Polly she'd have to reveal what had prompted it, which would presumably mean turning daughter against father, the father she adored. Could she, Julia, bring herself to do that? Probably not. Martin might deserve whatever pain disclosure caused him, but Julia couldn't bear to think of wounding her daughter. And suppose Polly resented, turned against her mother for her revelation? That thought was unbearable. She would have somehow to cope without involving Polly, find a way of insisting that the decision to visit

105

Brighton was a spur-of-the-moment whim, a fancy brought on by a twinge of envy, no more than that, at the thought of her husband's American adventure. The rest would be silence. She'd read newspaper accounts of wives who'd revenged themselves on their rattish husbands, and had laughed – good God, with Martin she'd laughed, they so often read the paper together – at the report of how one had cut off the right arm of all her husband's Savile Row suits; and she'd cheered – again, with Martin – at the account of how another poured away the contents of a cellarful of vintage wines. Could she behave like that? Could she?

She dried her hands, went upstairs and stood in her husband's study. Suppose she phoned the council for a skip, took out all his books and ordered their removal to a waste tip? No. Then how about ripping out pages from one book in ten? No, again. Could she perhaps deface certain books by scribbling in them at random? No, no, no. Childish petulance. To choose to damage a book was anathema to her. From early childhood she had been aware of the intensity of her mother's regard for the few books she possessed; they had an almost talismanic power for her, they were proof of redemption from ignorance, and she protected them from damage as a religious devotee would protect from harm a sacred relic.

So, no to that. You did not set yourself to desecrate books. Leave that to the idiots, religious fundamentalists, political ideologues, moral censors, who thought that the burning of books or their wilful destruction by other means would somehow rid the world of ideas too dangerous, or blasphemous, or wicked, to be permitted.

What then? Could she at least show Polly the note from Sandra and ask her daughter what she made of it? NO. Out of the question.

Julia left the study, shutting the door behind her. Shut not closed.

In her bedroom she snapped on the light and at once noticed, thrown on the made bed, the book she'd first read on the train to Brighton, and which she'd been looking into again as she dressed this morning. It was, she knew, open at the poem which, after several readings, she now had more or less by heart.

Though reason proves
Love deceives at every turn, hands back the ring, breaks every vow
Still our actions are compelled by it. It's all we own.

Love is all we own? No, she thought, reaching for the book and replacing it on her bedside table, it's love that owns us. We may not like it, but it's true. Our actions *are* compelled by it. All of them.

She turned off the light and went to stand by her uncurtained window, looking out at the September evening as it darkened to night. She was drawn there by the sounds of doors slamming as drivers and their passengers left cars that were being parked outside a house across the way. She watched as, gripping bottles and bunches of flowers, people walked up the drive, some skipping in their eagerness to join those indoors, others moving more demurely, all of them passing through the front-door's curtain of light into a peopled place where figures moved about what she knew was a long through room. The hosts were not friends of hers, nor did she wish that they might be. According to Muriel, the house-owners, newly arrived, wouldn't, so she had told Julia, be 'your kind of a person.' The man was a director of a furniture company, his wife – 'if that's what she is' – a buyer for one of the city's fashion stores. 'Treat themselves as Lord and Lady Muck.'

Closing her curtains, she turned on the bedroom light, pausing to look in turn at wardrobe, bed, chest of drawers, full-length mirror, trying to find comfort in their familiar appearances. They looked blankly back.

16

SATURDAY EVENING. POLLY MUST BE BACK by now. I was hoping she'd phone to let me know, but nothing so far. Probably tired by the journey up to London. Anyway it's given me time to consider what I'll tell her about Martin. What *can* I tell her? That her father has been unfaithful? How wersh it sounds. And suppose Polly thinks it no big deal. For god's sake, Mum – men – and women for that matter – have affairs. Get over it.

But he got a student of his pregnant and the girl killed herself. No, I can't tell Polly that, not, at least, until Martin is home again. I need to talk to him first, always supposing he's prepared to talk to me about something he's kept to himself all these years. But *has* he kept it to himself? Might he have confided in his male friends? Giles, for instance. *Could* he have talked to him on that occasion Tony Rayburn heard him lecture? Newly a professor and scared that, if news about why Sandra killed herself got out, his career would be on the line? Seeking advice from someone who was already a smooth operator, able to open and close doors. Giles, the manager, Giles, the proverbial safe pair of hands. 'Leave it to me, old boy.' I can hear Giles's voice. And now, maybe, he's calling in his debt, which is why he wants Martin to arrange an invitation to America for him.

No, that doesn't make sense. Why should Martin have anything to fear? Unless, of course, he thought there might be another note beside the one he'd hidden away? Perhaps he thought, perhaps he *knew*, that the poor girl had written to explain her decision to kill herself – though, if so, who had she written to, and how did Martin know about it? Did she tell him what she'd done? 'I'm sending X an account of our affair and I'm going to reveal to him/ her the name of the man whose child I'm carrying. Let's see you get out of *that*, Professor Gibbs.' So how did he?

Julia put down her pen, her hand shaking. My god, she thought, I can't put any more of this in writing, I can't even *think* it. Something Trudy had said when Julia had told her about the discovery of Sandra's note buzzed in her head. It could be that she'd cried wolf once too often. Sandra had expected Martin to come running, she meant, only this time he didn't. *I can't go on. Tomorrow will be too late.* He hadn't responded, and then it *had* been too late.

But it hadn't been Martin who discovered the body. As well as she was able, Julia set herself to recall the course of events covering Sandra's death and its aftermath. Martin was, wasn't he, at home when the phone call came to tell him that one of his students had killed herself, her body found by her landlady? Julia returned from college to be greeted by her husband desperate to tell her of the tragedy. He himself was in a state of what had seemed, no, surely *was,* bewildered distress. Sandra was, after all, someone he had often told his wife was a student of unusual promise, widely-read, prompt at completing her well-written assignments, always eager to challenge her lecturers' points of view if she felt they were dubious or plain wrong. He had made no bones about his admiration for her. 'She was outstandingly good,' he said. 'Easily the best of her year.' And in the days after her death, he made no attempt to hide his grief over what he repeatedly said was the girl's needless death.

'I simply don't understand it,' he told Julia one evening, after coming down from his nightly routine of chatting with the ten-year-old Polly about her day before he left her propped up in bed, one of her favourite books – Alan Garner, probably, or Richard Mayne – open for the half-hour reading she was permitted before either he or Julia went up to switch off her light. 'Such a terrible, terrible waste. All the love it takes to bring a new life into existence – and then for it to be snuffed out.' He was, Julia knew, thinking not merely of Sandra but, as she was, of their daughter, their only child, of Polly.

Even when the post-mortem revealed Sandra's pregnancy, Martin continued to express bewilderment as well as sorrow. 'Why didn't she talk to someone? If it was a boyfriend – or a one-night stand, for that matter – they could have arranged an abortion. No one would need to know. It must happen all the time on university campuses.'

'Perhaps she was a Catholic?' Julia suggested.

'If so, I'll find out tomorrow. Her parents are coming up from Somerset to meet Arthur and me. I'm not looking forward to that, I can tell you.' Arthur Howard was the Head of Department.

The following evening, when Julia asked him how the interview had gone, he seemed transfixed by sadness as he told her. 'It was awful.' He could say no more for some minutes, then, his own eyes full of tears, Martin explained how, a few moments after the parents had been ushered into Howard's office and gestured towards office chairs that had been placed side by side facing the desk behind which the Head of Department and Martin sat, 'like some sort of bloody Tribunal', Sandra's mother, grey-faced and rigid, almost immediately broke down, howling, rocking to and fro and slapping away her husband's arm as he knelt beside her trying to offer comfort. The man had looked apologetically across at Martin, but Martin, so he said, told him there was nothing to apologise for, that grief at such a time was unsurprising, and 'more I don't remember. Meaningless babble, I've no doubt. Words of comfort? There aren't any.'

Remembering now his account of Sandra's distraught mother, Julia remembered most vividly the look in Martin's eyes when he said that the meeting with the girl's parents had been probably the worst part of it – 'I can tell you.'

But what hadn't he told her?

Julia picked up her pen again.

'These deeds must not be thought/After these ways; so, it will make us mad.' But I am not Lady Macbeth, I *need* to think. Before he's back, *if* he comes back, if I allow him back into my life, I have to make as much sense as I can of what happened all those years ago. At the moment I could even believe he was responsible for her death.

She stared at the words. What on earth did she mean by them?

* * *

She was still labouring to understand when, half an hour later, her phone rang. But it wasn't Polly Julia found herself talking to. 'Hello, ducks.' The exuberance of Trudy's voice acted like a rush of warmth. 'How are you? Dreaming of far away places?'

'No,' Julia was laughing, in spite of herself. 'I'm thinking of matters close to hand. Next week's classes. And wondering when Polly is going to get in touch. They must be home by now.'

'Well, why not phone her when you've done with me? Meanwhile, I have a suggestion. Are you sitting comfortably?' And before Julia could reply, her friend rushed on, 'Here goes, then, and now I come to think of it, it's advice rather than suggestion. Drop everything and fly to San Francisco. You can be there and back in three or four days. James and I are going to New York next weekend – Friday to Monday. It's easy.'

'Easy for you,' Julia said. 'I'd not be allowed to take time off.'

'You wouldn't need to. Go online and you'll find tickets to get you there and back in a weekend. James agrees with me. I was knocked sideways, Julia, when you said you didn't want Martin back. I've been thinking about that all week. Especially when your letter came. Of course, I'm your friend, by the way. Hence my suggestion. Advice. Order.'

But Julia ignored Trudy's concern. 'James? *What* have you been telling him?'

'Hey, Julia,' Trudy said, 'friends we may be but there's no need to shout. I simply told him I was sorry – very sorry – that you and Martin seem to have parted on bad terms. I didn't say anything else, believe me.'

Julia was contrite. 'I do, and I apologise for shouting at you. But I can't get away, I simply can't.'

And I don't want to, she thought, when, after a few more desultory sentences, she wished her friend and James a good time in New York, and put the phone down. I can't face Martin, not yet, not until I know more about that girl's death.

She stood, went to the fridge, reached for the opened bottle. But no, she said to herself as she shut the fridge door – shut, not closed – that's not the solution. She would make herself some pasta.

All the same, she thought, measuring spaghetti into boiling water, how easy it was for Trudy to assume that her own new-found happiness could somehow gift her with the solution to other people's problems. I am happy, therefore I command you to be happy. It didn't work like that. Laughter now, that was different. Laughter not only could be shared, it invariably was. As she grated cheese over her plate of spaghetti she remembered an occasion when, waiting the overdue arrival of a train on some station or other, she'd been sitting in a crowded bar laughing at the opening page of a Wodehouse novel and when she looked up discovered that people were looking at her and that *all* of them were laughing. Should she apologise? But there was no call to be embarrassed. No wonder, she thought now, as she had thought then, laughter was so often called infectious. Not contagious, no, it didn't spread from bodily contact but simply from being in the same room as the person who'd laughed, sharing the atmosphere.

Misery didn't work like that. Laugh and the world laughs with you. Cry and you cry alone. Another of her mother's sayings, and, she acknowledged as she scooped up some strands of spaghetti, a wise old saw.

The phone rang and this time it *was* Polly.

'Wow,' Polly said. 'Do you know you're shouting?'

Julia laughed. 'You're the second caller to tell me that this evening.'

'The other being Dad, I guess.'

'No, a friend who thinks I ought to drop everything and fly to San Francisco to see your father.'

'Why? Is he ill or something?' Polly sounded startled.

I shouldn't have mentioned that, Julia thought. Idiot. 'No,' she said, speaking as lightly as she could. 'No, your father is fine. It was a friend. A recent friend, one you've not yet met. Do you remember James, James Piper? This is his latest conquest, Trudy Cosgrove, she's called, and this time I think it will last. He's apparently promised to make a respectable woman of her and she's light-headed on love and wants everyone else to breathe the same air. Even fly by it. I told her that some of us have work to go to.'

'Doesn't she have work, then? Or is she a kept woman? Honestly, Mum, the company you keep.' But Polly was laughing. Dear Polly.

'Trudy is younger than James by, I'd say, getting on for twenty years,' Julia told her daughter, 'but it may work, who knows? And, dear

112

daughter, in the short time I've known her, since we met when we were all on the island, she and I have become good friends – we get on like a house on fire, as your gran would have said. And, quaint old-fashioned thing that she is, she even calls me "ducks".' She decided not to mention the day she and Trudy had spent at Brighton.

'You mean she thinks *you're* old fashioned? What a nerve.'

'Not at all. Trudy is all gold.'

Polly said, 'In that case your friend James has struck lucky. Greybeard goes cradle snatching and gets away with it. Or her.' A laugh and with it James was dismissed. France was on Polly's mind.

But after some minutes in which she ran at speed through a list of towns and meals, sampled and enjoyed, Polly suddenly stopped. 'I don't want to tell you all this now,' she said, 'otherwise I'll have nothing left for when we meet. Al and I were thinking we'd come up next weekend. Would that be OK?'

'Of course it would.'

'You're shouting again,' Polly said. 'I'll let you know sometime next week when to expect us. Until then, Al sends love and so *of course* do I.' And the line went dead.

Julia sat at the table, unmoving, staring at her empty plate. Then she stood. She would do the washing up. She would not cry.

17

LOOKING OUT OF THE KITCHEN WINDOW as she stood, crunching through a slice of toast, Julia watched the last stains of the night sky fading into a clear Sunday morning.

She had slept well. The self-pitying mood of the previous evening was scrubbed clean. Later that day she would have to prepare for the coming week's classes but for now she was going to take herself for a walk.

From the hook on the back of the kitchen door she took a light jacket, first removing then replacing the raincoat Martin had bought that time the three of them spent an Easter weekend in Derbyshire. Getting on for twenty years ago, that must have been, a weekend of blustery showers, the cottage they had hired cosy and warm, so they had sung to their small daughter. We can weather the storm. But Polly preferred to be outside. She was entranced by the horses in the paddock beside the cottage, calling to them and then, when they lumbered over to where she stood and thrust their slobbery muzzles between the bars of the five-barred gate, squealing in joyous terror. Lifted into her mother's arms she quivered, stiff, dauntless, as their thick black lips snatched at the wisps of grass her father had gathered for her to offer them.

Odd, Julia thought, as she shrugged herself into her jacket, Polly, unlike most small girls, had never been interested in riding lessons. She preferred riding a bike and so, with her parents, and, later, friends of her own age, journeyed out along the local tow path, often for hours on end and then, in her pre-university summer, spent a week camping in

Shropshire with classmates. Her first time away from her parents, their first experience of the absence that in later years they came to identify with a recovered freedom but which at first they greeted as an ache of loss.

Glancing at her image in the hall mirror – blonde hair not yet losing out to grey – Julia checked she had her house keys, then, pulling to the front door, stepped out into the porch.

'Good morning, Julia.' Armed with the habitual shears, her neighbour came into view behind her side of the privet hedge.

Found any leaves to cut? Julia did not ask. Instead, she said, briskly cheerful, 'Good enough for a walk.'

'Going far?'

'There and back to see how far it is.' And she offered Muriel what she hoped was a disarming smile.

But as she waited at the bus stop, she thought, ruefully, I should really have found something more to say to her. She's lonely. Next time I'll stop for a chat. Though she doubted that she would.

Twenty minutes later she was picking her way along the rutted, stony track that led down to the river. In wet weather the track was so deeply puddled as to be impassable; but now, particles of what looked to be dust rose from the dry earth, particles she knew to be insects, a dance of atoms glittering in the autumn sun.

Coming out onto the river bank she saw a bird perched on the prow of a moored dinghy. The boat was some yards distant, among reeds that stuck out of the water like a palisade guarding some long gone dwelling, and the bird, big, scrawny, black, was staring fixedly into the water, wings hunched. A cormorant. On one of the walks they took as students along the Thames, Martin, who was knowledgeable about birds, had identified it for her. 'Unmistakeable,' he said, 'a clergyman's broken umbrella. That's all you need to remember. Anglers hate them, of course. My Dad used to take me fishing, though he spent most of his time chucking stones at any cormorant he saw trying to nick fish. Dace, chub, roach. All one to a cormorant.' He laughed. 'Secretly I was on the bird's side, though I never told my father.'

Years later, by which time she knew that cormorants were emblems of solitariness, Julia came across a poem which advised the reader to take heart from the bird's example. 'Turn your scarred back/On all who'd try/To offer you/Cold toad pie.'

'Not bad,' Martin said, 'though I don't think cormorants eat toads. Small frogs, yes.'

'Pedant,' Julia said.

Her reverie was interrupted by a cry.

'*Julia!*'

Turning, she saw a small motor boat some fifty or so yards upstream. Two men stood either side of the tiny cabin, waving at her, and as they came closer she recognised Graham Richards and his partner, Ronnie Nolan.

'Good morning, landlubber,' Graham called. He was in high good spirits. 'There's a mooring post a bit further on. We'll pull in and wait for you', and the boat chugged on its way.

By the time she reached the post, they were ashore, Graham's crumpled jeans and sweater no match for Ronnie's parody of nautical wear – blue-and-white hooped shirt, white bell-bottoms, shiny black shoes.

'Where's the parrot?' Julia asked him.

'At home, being sick,' Ronnie said. Then, 'Like it?'

'What, your get up?'

'The boat, my love.'

'Is it yours?'

They had to stand aside for a posse of cyclists to swoop past, before Ronnie could add, 'No criticism, *if* you please. I bought it with money an aged aunt left me.'

'Which explains the name, I take it.' Julia was looking at the letters painted in extravagant black on the boat's side. AUNTIE AGNES.

'Got it in one,' Graham said. He looked at Ronnie. 'Should we press-gang this lady and take her for a trip downstream?'

'A good idea,' Ronnie said. 'And there's a riverside pub where we could put in for lunch. Highly recommended in the Good Watering Hole Guide. Or we could simply go cruising.' And he fell about laughing.

'It's too early for lunch,' Julia said, 'but, yes, a boat trip would be fun.'

116

Her chance meeting with the two had cheered her, and as she followed them onto the boat, accepting Graham's hand to help her aboard, she said, giggling, 'It's like journeying into darkest England, isn't it? The Congo of the Midlands.'

Graham, who had taken the wheel, said, 'A desperate adventure. Just like The African Queen.'

'Speak for yourself,' Ronnie said.

***

Two hours later, by which time the two men had none too skilfully manoeuvred the boat some few miles down river, then brought it back upstream, they found a mooring space in front of a riverside pub. Getting the boat into the space took rather more time than seemed proper, but eventually they managed it, though as they scrambled up the river bank, a man, dressed as a biker, who was lounging with mates at a table in front of The Fisherman's Rest, said, 'Well done, lads, I knew you'd get there before dark. Got a licence for that cargo ship, have you?'

'I'll have you know that boat has been everywhere,' Ronnie said, mock offended. 'Dunkirk, Dieppe, you name it.'

'Derby?' But there was no malice in the biker's laughter, nor that of his mates. The day's benign warmth affected them all.

Once inside the pub, Graham took their orders then went over to the bar. While he was gone – he seemed to be in prolonged conversation with a man Julia took to be the landlord – Ronnie told her about what he called the rigmarole of buying the boat, then acquiring a licence and mooring rights. 'Then we had to paint it. I had to take time off work, if you please. Ladies hammering at my door, demanding their perms, and me laid up with decorator's disease.'

'What's that?'

'Spots before the eyes. Ah, here, and none too soon, is our tucker.'

Graham came to join them, bearing a tray on which were glasses of beer, and followed by a barman with a large plate of baguettes.

As they chewed, and swallowed ale, the two men chatted happily and with occasional hoots of laughter recounted for Julia's benefit various mishaps they had experienced with AUNTIE AGNES. If they noticed her silences they gave no hint of having done so. And anyway, as the meal went on, she joined with increasing readiness in their laughter.

And when Graham asked after Martin, how was he getting on in foreign parts, she said that he seemed happy enough.

'And the next thing you know, he'll be home,' Ronnie said, 'and you won't need us.' He pretended to sob.

'I'm having a lovely time with you,' Julia said. 'Really. Think I'll call you my two daffodils.'

'Charmed, I'm sure,' Ronnie said.

'Why?' Graham demanded.

'Because I can't but be gay in such a jocund company.'

'*You're* gay?'

But Ronnie's show of comic disbelief was cut off by the landlord, who now came to clear their plates and glasses and ask if there was anything else they required. And when they shook their heads, he said to Graham, 'Well, then, we'll see you next Friday, Mr Richards.'

'And what was that about?' Ronnie asked when the man had left them. 'Mr Richards? Are you known in these parts?'

'You know perfectly well,' Graham said, then to Julia, 'We've arranged a bit of a knees-up, a launch party for AUNTIE. Invite a chosen few and crack a bottle of Babycham over her bows. No brass band, but we can all sing.'

Standing, Ronnie said, 'And who better than Julia to bless our boat and all who sail in her? Will you do us and AUNTIE the honour?'

As she got to her feet, Julia said, 'I'd be honoured.'

* * *

Back home, still buoyant from her encounter with Graham and Ronnie, her two daffodils as she now thought of them, Julia took from the back room that served as her study books and papers she'd need for the coming week's teaching, and laid them out on the kitchen table. Despite everything, which meant despite the irritations and insufficiencies of being a part-timer, the petty snubs, despite people like Rudkin, she enjoyed teaching. There was reward enough to be found in those occasions of a student's gratified enlightenment. She remembered reading that the original meaning of 'pupil' came from the image of a teacher reflected back in a student's eye. She liked that.

IV

18

'*MUCH ADO ABOUT NOTHING?* WHAT'S THAT supposed to mean?'

Julia met the enquiring, slightly aggressive expression on the face of the youth who had asked the question, the same one who had elected to misunderstand the meaning of 'Paying Calls' – his name, she now knew, was Alistair Grenfell – with a question of her own. 'What do you *think* it means,' she asked, 'now that you've read the play?'

'Not a clue,' he said, 'Like Duncan here I thought *you* were supposed to tell *us*.' He pointed to the Chinese student then looked round more widely for support, and encouraged by the one or two of his friends who nodded agreement, said 'You're the teacher.'

Grenfell had chosen himself to be the class goad, Lord of Misrule, anything to raise a laugh.

Rule Number One of the Lecturer's Guide To Successful Class Management. Avoid confrontational situations. 'Can anyone help Alistair out of his difficulty?' Julia asked.

An girl raised her hand. 'Making a mountain out of a molehill,' she said.

'Very good, Indira,' Julia said.

'What's a molehill?' Rodney said.

'I know the answer to that,' a youth sitting behind Grenfell said. 'A pile of dirt.' He paused. 'Like Alistair.'

There was some sniggering, which Julia overrode by saying, 'I suggest we try to concentrate on the play itself, especially the relationship between Benedick and Beatrice.'

'Yeah, well, that's a load of ado about nothing,' Alistair said.

'Oh, for Christ's sake shut up,' Julia said.

* * *

In the Royal Oak, where some of them met early that evening, Julia reported her run-in with Grenfell. 'To be honest,' she said when she finished, 'I was half expecting Janine to call me in. I thought he'd probably complain about being disrespected.'

'I know him,' Andy Jenkins said. 'He's trouble. I've had him for two classes so far and already I want to defenestrate the sod.'

'A suitable case for counselling, young Grenfell,' someone said, satirically. 'You see, that'll be how management explain him. Low self-esteem, disadvantaged background, blah, blah.'

Graham, who had joined them in time to hear the name of Grenfell mentioned, said, 'His dad's a self-made millionaire.' He swallowed a mouthful of beer, gazed appreciatively at the glass he was holding aloft, said, 'By gum, lad, you needed that', before adding, 'Property. Buys cheap, sells dear, that's Grenfell for you. I guess Son will follow him into the business.'

'Why is he at college, then?' Julia said. 'He's not interested in what I teach, that's for sure. I wish he'd clear off.'

* * *

Which, in a manner of speaking, he did. The following morning, when Julia entered the staff room, she found a note in her pigeon-hole asking her to 'attend' the college secretary's office 'at your earliest opportunity', and after a full morning's teaching presented herself outside the office's glazed door. As she made to knock she glanced at the gold lettering above the glass. DAVID RUDKIN, BA, SECRETARY. That was new, surely?

'Come.' The secretary, in pin-stripe suit, white, stiff-collared shirt and tightly-knotted tie, did not invite her to take a seat. Behind his desk, at which he sat bolt upright, he scrutinised her silently and at some length.

Finally, he said, 'I regret to inform you that I have received further evidence of that lessening of interest in your subject among students of which I had reason to speak when we last met.' Looking mightily pleased to have emerged triumphant from the syntax of that sentence, he added after a pause, 'You are doubtless familiar with the name of Alistair Grenfell?'

'Unfortunately, yes.'

The secretary sniffed. 'He has expressed a wish to transfer from English studies to History.'

'What have History done to deserve that?'

'He complained about your attitude to him. He felt his tutor, that is you, was ... '

'Don't tell me,' Julia said. 'Was disrespecting him.'

' ... was not sufficiently fructifying.'

'*Fructifying!* Grenfell used the word fructifying?'

'That, I admit, is my term.' The secretary looked even more pleased with himself.

'Congratulations,' Julia said.

And for the rest of the week she felt that she herself was due congratulations, because in the absence of Grenfell her teaching became a pleasure, and this, even though she couldn't persuade her class of the value attached to Beatrice and Benedick's 'reasonable love'.

'Why wait around? You could be dead next week,' one youth said. And a woman student agreed with him. 'Suppose Benedick hadn't come back from the war,' she argued, 'or Claudio had been killed before he met Hero?'

Julia wanted to argue back that the play took account of such misfortunes, that much ado might have amounted to a great deal, but instead she asked the students if they themselves felt the urge to seize the moment. And when they nodded and said yes, and one repeated that you could be dead next week, she wondered about them. They seemed so resigned, fatalistic, even. It wasn't cynicism. It was deeper, a kind of lassitude of soul. That wasn't how the young should be, was it? I'm getting old, she thought.

She was still preoccupied with thinking about the class's response to Shakespeare's play when, stepping onto the bus taking her to the christening party for AUNTIE AGNES, she was waved to by Tony Rayburn, already on board.

As she joined him, he looked approvingly at her tailored jeans and green linen jacket bought the previous day. 'We must be going in the same direction,' he said. 'I've come straight from college. No time to change.'

'You'll do,' Julia said, glancing at his jacket and the dark blue trousers. Men, even on formal occasions, and even the scruffiest of them, could get away with casual dress. Besides, there was an easy grace about the way Rayburn wore his clothes. For something to say, 'Are you still enjoying teaching here?' she asked.

He had been peering out of the window, watching the river as the bus rumbled along beside it. Slowly, he turned back to her. 'That lad Grenfell,' he said.

Julia sighed. 'What about him?'

'I can't make him out. I know he joined my group because you and he didn't get on, but he doesn't seem any more interested in History than in Literature. He's not a fool but he likes playing one. What's he up to? I get the impression he's one of a protected species.' After a moment, Rayburn said, twisting in his seat to look at her, 'Rudkin tells me his father can cause difficulties for the college.'

So Rudkin had been warning Tony Rayburn not to repeat her mistake, had he? No doubt he'd invited Rayburn in for a man-to-man conversation, probably let drop that the part-time lecturer in English showed, alas, all the signs of menopausal imbalance and would have to be watched carefully for further indications of unreasonable behaviour. She was trying to decide whether to probe Rayburn on what Rudkin had said when she realised they were nearing their stop. It would have to wait.

They crossed the road and walked the short distance to The Fisherman's Rest, passing as they did so numerous cars and vans parked along the grassy verge. Sounds of live music came from behind the pub, and as Julia and Tony, having negotiated a way through the already crowded saloon bar, emerged onto the terrace above the river bank, they were able to watch a trio of musicians, who had just finished playing a number, bow ironically to party-goers standing around in small groups, talking and shouting among themselves.

'Who are they?' Julia asked a woman standing next to her. Her question was answered by the black, formidably-built guitarist who now announced that The Terry Marsden Quartet Minus Terry Marsden would be taking a break. 'No need for panic, though,' he said. 'We'll be back to spread a little happiness just as soon as we've recovered from the excitement of the first set.'

'Are they good?' Julia asked.

The woman looked sceptically at her. 'If you like that kind of thing,' she said. She evidently didn't.

Julia and Tony made their way over to a huddle of college staff, most clutching wine glasses, though Andy Jenkins held aloft a beer tankard as a form of greeting.

'Good,' he said loudly into Julia's ear. 'Now you're here the official part of the evening can commence. Graham and Ronnie are down by the boat. You're not planning to make a long speech I hope?'

'I shan't be making *any* speech,' Julia said, laughing as she saw Graham, from below the terrace, beckon to her. He was waving a bottle aloft and mouthing words which, she surmised, formed a request to join him so they could undertake the ceremony.

'I don't suppose there'll be any brass band music,' Tony said, as he followed Julia down towards the river, and Andy, accompanying them, said, 'Fat chance. "Abide With Me" from a jazz trio?'

Putting an arm round Julia, Graham kissed her on the cheek, then, swivelling, shouted to the many guests now spilling off the terrace, 'All aboard the Skylark! Hurry, Hurry! Julia is about to christen our boat!' He let go of her in order to wrench the cork from out of the bottle of Prosecco. 'A libation is all that's required,' he ordered. 'I've promised the landlord there'll be no broken glass.'

A large crowd was now gathered, some on the path, others on the grass, as Julia stepped forward to pour wine over the boat's bow, 'But where's Ronnie?' she asked.

'You'll see,' Graham said.

Julia tipped the bottle up, watched as the foamy liquid spread across the front of the boat and said, 'I name this ship AUNTIE AGNES', and as she did so and to the accompaniment of laughter and applause, the door to the tiny cabin abruptly opened and Ronnie, dressed as a pantomime dame, flounced into view. He waved his wand, a lavatory brush with tinsel star, said something Julia could barely hear about the healing spirit of the river, then clambered into the stern from where he jumped into the shallow water and began splashing the nearest spectators. Screams, yells of 'Give over, Ronnie!' and the crowd retreated and scrambled back to safety.

On the terrace, the trio began to play a tune Julia recognised as 'Red Sails in the Sunset'.

'Not bad, are they?' Tony said when the number came to an end, but he was the only person to applaud.

* * *

'What time does this place close?' Tony asked Julia. It was late, late in the evening, most of the christening party had long since disappeared, and while the remaining drinkers were mostly clustered at the bar, she and Tony were, as they had been for the past half hour, sitting at a small table at the back of the room. He had been asking her about Grenfell senior. What did she know about him? Not much, she said, apart from the fact that he had deep pockets and was an influential city councillor, after which she had fallen silent as Tony speculated aloud about the likelihood of Grenfell being able to 'lean on' the college governors, and, further speculation, if so, whether his son might be someone to watch out for.

'Sorry,' Julia said through a yawn. She was suddenly very tired.

It was then Tony asked his question about when the pub closed, and followed it with another. 'More importantly, when does the last bus go?'

Julia peered at her watch. 'We'll need to order a taxi,' she said.

'Time for another, then.'

But Julia shook her head. She'd already drunk more than she was used to, and sometime tomorrow morning Polly and Al were due. Not too early, Polly had promised when she'd phoned the previous evening to confirm arrangements, but in good time for lunch. And in reply to a further question from her mother she'd said, 'Oh, a sandwich and a cup of tea will do. We want to take you out for dinner. You book somewhere, and Al and I will stand treat.'

Now, Julia suddenly realised she'd forgotten to obey her daughter's request. Damn. Well, tomorrow morning then.

Standing none too steadily in the women's toilets, Julia peered at her image in the mirror. Beside her a much younger woman leant forward to apply lipstick and, meeting Julia's reflected gaze, said, 'Don't know why I bother, really. He's too pissed to notice.' Then, grinning, 'Still, he's not too pissed to get what he's paid for.' And in a swirl of scent she snapped her handbag shut and left, saying as she did so, 'Good luck.'

'Good luck'. What did *that* mean? Julia wondered as she and Tony waited for their taxi to arrive, the night air still warm though a momentary whisper of chill wind caused her to shiver. Without speaking, Tony took off his jacket and held it out to her, but she shook her head. And when the taxi at last arrived she made sure to sit well to her side of the back seat, staring ahead at the back of the driver's head, determined to keep awake.

'Where we going then?'

The words startled her out of her slumbrous state.

Realising that it was the driver had spoken, Julia leant forward and gave him her address, then she leant back and closed her eyes.

Some time later, she was aware of Tony shaking her by the shoulder. 'Julia, we're here.'

Keen to prove that she was wakeful, alert, she opened her door abruptly, half-fell from the taxi, and, trying to right herself, jammed her foot against the kerb and toppled face down onto the pavement.

A moment later she felt hands beneath her armpits and Tony's voice, urgent with concern, 'Julia, Julia, are you alright? No, don't try to get up, not until you've got your breath.'

Shrugging herself free of his hands, she levered her body up and swung round into a sitting position. By now the taxi driver was standing beside Tony's crouching figure, both of them illuminated by a nearby street lamp.

'I tripped,' she said, aware of the shakiness of her voice. She took a deep breath, let it out and said, slowly, to give her vision time to clear, 'I'm so sorry. I must get indoors.' She was suddenly feeling sick.

'Let me help you.' Tony took an elbow but she winced away from him. 'Does it hurt?'

Julia managed to get to her feet, swayed and almost fell again. She put her hands up to cover her face, said, 'A minute, that's all I need.' The feeling of nausea was retreating but the shaking wouldn't stop. Her right ankle was throbbing. She tried putting weight on it, drew in breath and bit her lip, using the back of her hand to wipe her eyes.

To the driver Tony said, 'Help me get her across the road, will you?' and the two men, placing arms round her waist, half-carried, half-eased her over the road.

As the three of them stood outside her darkened front door, Julia reached into her jacket and handed Tony her house-keys.

He fumbled to match key to lock and at last the door swung open. She leant against the door frame, aware that Tony was handing money to the driver, and hearing his words. 'Give me your card. I'll stay with her until I know she's alright.'

A moment later, hand under the unhurt elbow, he was helping her into her hallway, heeling the front door shut behind him.

She sat on a kitchen chair, examined her torn jeans, the scuff marks on the sleeve of her jacket. I will not cry, she told herself. She studied Tony's bent head, his cropped brown hair as, prising off her shallow, flat-soled boot, he knelt to examine her ankle. His fingers on her ankle bone were disturbingly gentle. This way, that, they went, before, raising himself onto his knees, he said, 'Bruised but not broken, I'd say. You need a cold compress.'

'Thank you, Doctor.'

'You're welcome.' He smiled up at her. 'I did a basic course in first aid at university. It came in useful when I played student football.'

'Is football a violent game?'

Grinning, he shook his head. 'Not the way I played it. But even in a Sunday morning kick-about, you can still dream. Sprinting down the middle of a churned-up meadow at half-a-mile an hour you're really Gazza or the Boy Beckham. And then you smack into some hung-over sod who knows he's really Roy Keane. And you both end up in the mud, a heap of twisted limbs like a mini-battle of the Somme. That's when first-aid comes in handy.'

He was trying to put her at her ease.

He got to his feet. 'I'll make you a cup of tea. Hot and sweet. Show me – no, tell me – where everything is.'

While he was squeezing out tea-bags at the sink, Julia struggled up from her chair. 'I need the loo,' she said.

He swung round. 'How are you going to get upstairs?'

'There's one downstairs. No, I can manage,' she said hastily, as he opened his mouth.

Locking the lavatory door, she stood stock still for a moment before slowly lowering her ripped jeans, then her pants, and, sweating, sat painfully to pee. As she washed her hands she looked into the mirror, saw her face, puffy from her tears, its strained pallor. 'Good luck,' she muttered with savage irony to her image.

***

Before he left her, Tony, having first run cold water into the washing-up bowl and placing her injured foot in it, went upstairs in order to find, under her shouted instructions, bandages in the bathroom cupboard, and a packet of painkillers. 'Where do you keep spare bedding?' he shouted down, and, to avoid possible misunderstanding, 'I'll need to make you a bed downstairs.'

He came into the kitchen, bedding in his arms, and, in his hands, a crepe bandage plus toothpaste and a toothbrush still in its wrapping. 'I'll make the bed first,' he said, and a few minutes later was back, the front room now a field hospital, so he said, grinning as he came towards her.

Once more he knelt, dried the injured foot, let the bandage unspool through his fingers, wrapped it round her ankle then down and under the sole, his movements comforting, deft, until, to finish with, and after delaying his work to answer some question she put to him, he tucked in the end of the bandage and the forcing movement made her momentarily cry out.

He looked up at her then. 'Sorry,' he said, 'I didn't mean to hurt you.'

She was, she knew, looking shocked, though it wasn't the touch of his fingers that had so affected her.

There was a knock on the front door.

'My taxi,' he said, scrambling to his feet.

At the kitchen door, he paused, looked back at her. 'I'm so sorry your evening ended so badly,' he said, and she thought he meant it. 'Look after yourself. You'll probably be able to hobble into college on Monday.'

A moment later she heard the front door open and quietly click shut.

Shut not closed, she thought as she hobbled into the front room and lowered herself, fully dressed, beneath the sheet and duvet Tony had draped over the sofa.

Lying in the dark, lights from an occasional passing car fingering the closed curtains, Julia tried to find a position in which she could rest comfortably. Inching her injured ankle free of the duvet's weight, she went over as much as she could recall of Tony's talk as he waited and watched, until, certain he had no need to call an ambulance – no concussion, no broken bones – he phoned for a taxi to take him back to his flat.

Her daughter was due to arrive in the morning, she assured him, and if there was an emergency, though there wouldn't be, she could summon her next-door neighbour. And she held up her mobile which he'd placed on the table beside her. Then, 'Ought you to let anyone know where you are?' she asked.

'I live alone,' Tony said. Leaning against the kitchen sink, jaw beginning to blur with dark overnight stubble, he sipped from the mug of tea he'd made for himself. He jerked his head upright, looked at her, his smile becoming a wry grimace. 'I used to be married. But ... '

'But that was in another country.'

Under the kitchen's strip lighting he stared at her. 'How did you know that?'

'I didn't,' she said. 'I'm sorry, it was a quotation. I didn't mean to ... to be intrusive.'

She wasn't sure that was the right word, but Tony accepted her hesitant apology with a quick nod. 'Well,' he said, 'there's nothing to hide.' And he spread his hands. 'Early marriage, early divorce. It happens all the time. Alice and I were at uni together then, after graduation, we decided to travel. VSO work, followed by a year wandering around Eastern Europe. We got married in Bulgaria. After that, I wanted to come back, begin research – I'd applied for and been given a scholarship – but Alice chose to see out a six-month contract she had, teaching at a language school in Romania. She said she'd follow, but soon after I'd returned I got a Dear John letter.'

While he spoke, back partly turned to her, he was running cold water into the bowl he then brought over, and he watched attentively as Julia slowly moved her injured foot about the bowl, the water a comfort to her throbbing ankle.

It was while he was bandaging her foot – wasn't it? – and after she'd swallowed a couple of the painkillers, that she asked him where he enrolled as a research student.

'Not where I wanted,' he said shaking his head, as, crouching, he lifted her foot, dried it, and began to apply the bandage. 'I wrote to your husband, asking if I could come to work with him, but he told me he was already over-committed. Well, no surprise there. So I went back to where I started.'

'To Giles – Professor Poynter?'

Tony nodded, sat back on his heels in order to look at her. 'He told me I was in luck. By great good fortune he was able to take me on. The impression he gave was that he was in endless demand but out of the kindness of his heart he'd squeeze in one more research student.'

Julia said, 'Lucky indeed.'

'Wasn't I just?' Tony's answering smile hinted at the sardonic. 'Still, he looked after me well enough, I'll give him that. Apparently, he'd been hoping – or assuming – that one of your husband's graduands would go to work with him. But that didn't pan out.'

Julia looked at him. 'Oh, why not? What went wrong? Didn't he want to work with Giles Poynter?'

'Not *he*,' Tony said, 'It was a woman.' He shrugged his shoulders. 'I don't know, though I did hear a rumour that there'd been some kind of setback, quite a serious one, so I heard.'

And at that moment they heard the knock on the door and, after his brief farewell, Tony was gone.

***

When she woke dawn light was edging the curtains. The painkillers had let her sleep. But as she emerged into wakefulness, aware of the throbbing of her ankle, she knew she needed to phone Trudy. Trudy who had queried, perhaps even disbelieved, Julia's account of what had happened twelve years ago, the very time when Tony Rayburn would have been beginning his research under Giles. 'There'd been some kind of setback, quite a serious one.' There had indeed. Tony's words explained it all. Martin must have tried to get the poor girl passed onto Giles.

Though I wonder how much Giles knew? she thought. Martin could well have told him no more than that he had a bright student, keen to go on to research, who would benefit from a change of place. Different voices, unfamiliar ideas, new intellectual challenges. Blah, blah. Giles would fall for it, of course. But *had* Sandra been a star in the making? Or had Martin tried to bribe the poor girl by suggesting she went somewhere else, knowing – well, guessing – that his friend would be only too pleased to take on one of Martin's students? Giles would love the idea of her preferring to study under him than under Martin. God, how he'd preen himself on *that*. And Giles above all people would know how to get his hands on a grant, not much doubt about it.

But then Sandra killed herself.

19

WHEN SHE NEXT WOKE IT WAS to a banging in her head.

No – someone was knocking on the front door.

Polly!

Julia swung her body up from the sofa, made to stand, cried out in pain.

Polly was now banging on the curtained window. 'Mum, are you in there? Mum! Can you hear me?'

'A minute,' she tried to shout back though her voice was little more than a croaky whisper. She hobbled across to the door, switched on the light, saw the crumpled heap of bedding, and switched the light off again. 'Coming,' she called, her voice stronger now, and limped to the front door.

Polly and Al stood in the porch, Al's smile uncertain, Polly's expression one of open alarm.

Concern in her eyes, her voice fretful with anxiety, she asked 'Mum, what's the matter? You look dreadful.' She stepped into the hallway, Al close behind her, edging past Julia as if he were scared to come within touching distance.

Julia closed the front door, turned to where the two were lined up, side by side, backs pressed to the lower banisters of the hall staircase, almost as though they were errant children called to the head teacher's study. That gave her a measure of control, and she smiled, a small, cracked smile, as she said 'I'm sorry. I'd no idea it was so late.'

She limped past them towards the kitchen. 'I'll make some tea,' she said as they followed her, 'or would you prefer coffee?' She motioned them to sit.

Polly pointed at her mother's strapped ankle. 'What on earth's happened?' she asked. 'You look as if you've been in a fight.'

Julia followed the direction of her daughter's look and it was only then that she realised she was still dressed in the clothes she'd worn the previous evening, including the ripped, muddied jeans, and her now much-crumpled blouse.

She put a hand up to her tousled hair. 'God,' she said, 'what a mess I'm in.'

If Polly sensed some deeper meaning in the seemingly trivial utterance she gave no sign of having done so. She stood up, said to her mother, 'Sit here. I'll run upstairs and get you some clean clothes and while you're using the downstairs shower, Al and I can make coffee for us all. Then we can talk.' Meaning, Julia knew, then you can tell us how you got in this state.

Which, some fifteen minutes later, freshly-showered, and, though sore at shoulder and elbow and unwilling to put much pressure on her injured ankle, now dressed in the loose sweater and skirt Polly had thoughtfully provided for her, she did. Her accident in tripping as she emerged from the taxi was, she emphasised, pure chance, though she was grateful a colleague was with her at the time.

'Who was that?'

'Nobody you'd know,' Julia told her daughter, 'he's new to the college.'

She decided not to mention Tony Rayburn's ministrations. 'But,' she added, making light of it, 'here's a strange coincidence. He was once a student of Giles Poynter.' She lifted the cup of black coffee Al had poured her. 'Giles and we – Polly's Dad and I – were students together.'

'Not much of a coincidence,' Polly said. 'I seem endlessly to bump into people who were at one time or another taught by Dad.' She paused. 'Speaking of which,' she said, 'his last text message to me suggested he thought you were rather overdoing things.'

'Really? What can he mean by that?' Julia tried not to sound startled.

'He didn't say. Working too hard, perhaps? I thought *you'd* know.'

Scraping back his chair, Al stood. Looming above the two women in what Julia thought must be his dressed-for-the-country gear of open-necked check shirt and brown cords, he said, 'I'm going to stroll down to the nearest newsagents. I need to straighten up from the journey. Two hours in a car bent like a hairpin is hard on a man.' But he was grinning. 'Is there anything I can get you, Julia, any shopping you need done?'

Understanding his tact in choosing to leave mother and daughter alone for a while, Julia shook her head, and as she heard the latch snap back and the front door close behind him, she said to Polly, smiling, 'You've chosen well, my darling daughter.'

'And you chose well, my darling mother. You and Dad ... ' Polly was watching Julia closely.

This is the moment, Julia thought. This is when I should tell her.

But even as she reached across the table and took Polly's hand in her own, she knew that she wouldn't. Couldn't. Wordlessly, she looked at her daughter, Polly's warm clasp a mute reassurance.

Indicating her mother's strapped ankle, Polly asked, 'Does Dad know about your accident?'

Julia shook her head. 'Not yet. Anyway, it's still the middle of the night in San Francisco. I'll text him later.'

'Wouldn't it be better to speak to him?' Polly's look was one of puzzlement, even, perhaps, reproof.

'Oh, I don't need to go that far.' Julia hardly knew what she was saying. Emptying her cup, she said, 'A phone call might alarm him. And by the time he's back in England I'll be right as rain.'

Still looking dubious, Polly said, 'Well, if you think so. It seems a bit odd to me ... '

She stood, gathered up their cups and took them across to the sink. 'The next time I speak to Dad I'll let him know that I've seen you and that you're one of the walking wounded.' She laughed. 'Helped in your hour of need by a protege of his friend, Giles.'

Julia said, sharply, 'I'd rather you didn't say anything about that.' Then, as Polly swung round from her rinsing of the cups to stare at her mother, she added as though in explanation, 'I'd rather not drag our friends into this.' Which made, she knew, no sense whatsoever. From

Polly's point of view, what harm could there possibly be in reporting the fact of Tony Rayburn having been Giles's student? All her outburst had achieved was to make her daughter think that maybe, just maybe, her mother was involved with him. Why else was he sharing her taxi? Was this, Polly must now be thinking, what her father had implied when he'd suggested that Julia was overdoing things? Her reluctance to phone him, her air of remoteness when they did speak, all added up to, could be interpreted as evidence of a ... of a ... God, she thought, what irony. Martin's the one who had an affair and I'm the one who's being accused.

Having dried her hands on a tea towel, a matter to which she gave considerable attention, Polly returned to face her mother across the breakfast table. 'Are you *sure* you're alright, Mum?'

Julia's laugh sounded to her own ears a brittle thing. 'You want to know whether I hit my head when I fell out of the taxi and whether I've gone doolally, is that it?'

For a moment, seeing the distress in Polly's eyes, she was tempted to tell her daughter everything, let her know about Sandra Hutchinson, about how, she now understood, Martin and Giles had between them plotted to get the student away from Martin and how their plan had gone wrong when she killed herself. Should she?

'Tell me about your holiday in France,' she said to Polly. 'I want to hear about all you did, all you saw.'

Perhaps startled into eloquence by the almost frantic urgency of her mother's request, Polly was still talking when they heard the front door open, and Al came into the kitchen, bearing a carrier bag from which he took what he called a lost timber-yard of Saturday papers and spread them on the kitchen table before crossing to the fridge where he crouched, looking to find room for a bottle of champagne he had extracted from the bag.

As he straightened up, he looked from mother to daughter, their hands clasped across the table, and said to Polly, 'Have you told your mother already?' There was a note of mild reproof in his voice.

'Of course not,' Polly said, 'I was waiting for you to return.'

'Tell me what?'

'We're thinking of re-locating,' Polly said.

138

'Not thinking, we *are*.' Al's voice was gentle but insistent.

'Oh, where to?' As she spoke, hope flared. Might they be leaving London to live somewhere nearer?

'New York,' Polly said, squeezing her mother's hand.

***

That evening they went out to celebrate. Julia's ankle was, she insisted, better. The swelling had gone down, the pain was beginning to fade, and, she told them, 'I can manage short walks as long as I'm not required to hurry.' She took with her a thick walking-stick, once her father's.

'Remember this?' she asked her daughter, holding it aloft as they left the house.

'Of course I do,' Polly said. 'Dad used to bring it with him when we went on country walks.' And to Al, as he helped her mother into the car, she said, 'We used to call it the Great Blackberry Catcher.'

'That came from your grandfather,' Julia said, settling herself into the passenger seat. 'I can still remember how he'd lecture me on not eating too many blackberries. "We don't want you in bed with the collywobbles."'

'No change there, then,' Polly said. 'It was what you told *me*.'

As they drove, mother and daughter reminisced about the family rambles of Polly's childhood – 'rambles in search of brambles' Polly said – and Julia told Al about how the small Polly, when denied further blackberries, would throw occasional tantrums, sometimes hurling herself to the ground in howls of violent protest, once, indeed, cutting her forehead on a shard of flint so that for a week afterwards she was forced to go around with her head bandaged and was, indeed, upset when the bandage was finally removed. Among her friends, it had made her a figure to be envied. 'Why can't *I* have a bandage?' some had asked.

Julia was laughing as she told the story. But she stopped short. For that small, histrionic daughter, whose pudgy hands once clasped trustingly round her mother's neck as she was carried to bed, was now the sleekly elegant, independent young woman, who with the tall, equally elegant man steering the car towards their chosen restaurant, would soon be 're-locating' thousands of miles away.

And this, Julia thought as they were shown to their table, was the cause of their celebration. But she tried to enjoy the couple's high spirits, their evident delight in each other and the future they planned. These were further advanced than she had expected. They were seeing out their contracts in London and would be free of them early in the New Year, when the lease on their flat also expired. Already, they had applied for work visas in America, were assured of two years' work in a New York agency whose London branch had recommended them, and this would give them time enough to decide whether to make a more permanent commitment to America.

'And commitment to each other, I take it?' Julia said, prodding at the grilled scampi she had let Al choose for her, as he had the other dishes in the tapas bar he'd also chosen once she admitted she'd forgotten to make restaurant reservations.

'Mum, you don't have to eat what you don't like,' Polly said, laughing. 'There's plenty to choose from.' She leant her head against her boyfriend's shoulder. 'Except when it comes to Al. He's the only oyster in my stew.' Which was, Julia assumed, as much of an answer to her implied question as she could expect.

A thought, no, a thrill of dread, ran through her. What about Martin? Had Polly told her father? Julia couldn't bear the possibility that he might already know of his daughter's plans. She nearly sighed aloud with relief when, as more dishes came to the table, Polly said, 'I shan't say anything to Dad until he's back here, safe and sound.' She forked up a slice of marinated fish. 'Al and I want to visit again once he's home. Don't we?' She spoke as though prompting him to utter lines he'd forgotten, and Al said, 'Of course we do.' He chewed, swallowed, said, 'Once we're in New York dropping in for a weekend won't be so easy.'

'No,' Julia said, 'it won't.'

'Mum,' Polly said, 'you're not enjoying this very much, are you?'

'Well ... ' Julia began, and hesitated.

'We should have gone to an Italian place,' Polly said. 'I'm so sorry. We

140

were hoping ... We wanted to make this a happy occasion.' Her voice was full of contrition.

I'm spoiling their evening, Julia thought. I ought to be happy for them, happy in their happiness. 'It's nothing.' she said, 'My ankle is hurting rather more than I thought it would, that's all.' Then, with determined brightness, she added, 'Nothing that a little more wine won't put right.' And as Al, who was driving, put a hand over his glass, she held out hers for Polly to re-fill.

* * *

The couple left before lunch the next day. Julia insisted on accompanying them to their car. 'I need to exercise my ankle,' she told them, 'ready for college tomorrow', and when Polly asked her wouldn't she be better taking a day or two off she insisted she'd be fine.

As they walked down the drive in cloudy sunshine they were hailed by the next-door neighbour, as always, it seemed, clipping her front hedge. They paused to exchange a polite word or two and Julia risked announcing that Polly and Al had come for the weekend and brought good news with them, though she decided not to reveal what that was.

Not that Muriel seemed greatly interested. 'I see you're limping,' she said, pointing with her shears at Julia's ankle, its strapping showing beneath the leg of her jeans.

'I took a tumble on Friday evening,' Julia said. 'Fell from a taxi, would you believe? I had to be helped indoors.' There was surely no harm in telling her that much.

'Ah,' Muriel said. 'Was that why that taxi was here so late? Must have been near on two o'clock. I got out of bed to see what was going on.' She looked enquiringly at Julia. 'Was that a doctor I saw leaving?'

'No.' Julia knew her cheeks were reddening. 'A colleague. We'd been at a party.'

Quickly turning away, she led Polly and Al down the drive.

As she watched them store their overnight bags in the boot of their shared VW, then come to embrace her, she said, 'Muriel's an incurable Nosey Parker.'

141

'I'd have liked to thank her for her help,' Polly said, her words hinting at mild reproof. And when Julia looked puzzled, she added, 'When you were in Brighton? She came round to see whether you were alright, didn't she? And left you a message, remember?'

'I've already thanked her,' Julia said briskly. 'But I'm happy to thank her again, on your behalf.'

A moment later they had ducked into their seats and Polly, winding down her window, called out, 'Take care of yourself, *please*, Mum', and the car began to roll.

* * *

Sunday evening. An awful weekend. A party on Friday evening that ended with me falling out of a taxi and damaging my ankle, after which I learn from the man who patched me up that my husband tried to palm off on to a friend the girl he'd made pregnant; and then, the following day, yesterday, a visit from Polly, so longed for, who told me that she and Al are off to New York, from which I now fear they're never likely to return. And to top it all off, as I was saying goodbye to them this morning, my neighbour pops up to let them know she saw a man leaving the premises in the wee small hours before their arrival. It was like one of those old Whitehall farces my parents used to enjoy, except that if you're in it rather than watching, it doesn't feel at all funny. And how could I explain that there was nothing amiss in Tony's being on the premises? I couldn't, but I saw their faces, Polly's especially. *What's* Mum been up to?

My darling daughter, I wish I could find a way of telling you that I've been up to nothing. Would I have felt better if there had been something to explain? Who knows? I do know there was that first impression, when Tony Rayburn and I were talking at the Royal Oak, and I did, I admit, let myself wonder about him. But our later meetings scotched *that*. Friendship was all he had on offer. And yet his touch, Tony's touch, when he was bandaging my ankle ...

Touch. Since my daughter and her partner left earlier today, I've been thinking about that. The need for it, the *yearning* for it. Polly holding my hand while we talked yesterday. I could have wept. When she was little she slipped her hand into mine each time we went out, even if we were going no further than the garden gate. And that time she had a friend to tea and the little girl – Rebecca I think she was called – asked Polly 'Did Mr Warner smile at you today?' – Mr Warner was their teacher – and in reply to Polly's saying yes, he did, Rebecca said 'He didn't smile at me,' and all the sadness of the world sounded through her words, so that Polly got down from her chair and went to put an arm round her friend. Fancy never being touched. That famous line needs re-writing. Not to have touch – not fire – is to be a skin that shrills. My skin shrills from the nearness of someone I want to touch but can't. Doesn't everyone's? That cliché, you hear it all the time. 'I was touched by your kindness.' 'It was a touching scene.' People don't mean it literally, but perhaps they should. Touchy, feely. Creeping Jesuses. No, I don't want to be touched by those who have designs on my soul. But Greeks repeatedly make physical contact, men as well as women. Hug, stroke each other, put an arm round a neck, a shoulder, round a waist, hold hands. You see it on the beach, but also when people are in the street. The common touch!

She set down her pen, sat thinking in the semi-dark of an early October evening. In a week Martin would be home and she still had no idea what to do. Would she be here when he arrived? *Would* he arrive? Or might he ... but no, for him, it was life as usual. It was for *her* that everything had changed.

She limped over to the fridge, poured herself some wine, and returned, bottle in one hand, glass in the other, to her chair. What she needed was someone to talk to, and that person couldn't be Polly. At moments during her daughter's visit she had dared to wonder whether she might risk bringing up the suicide of Martin's student and then, depending on Polly's reaction, find a way of hinting at its possible causes, but no. Polly, a young teenager at the time of the suicide, had inevitably heard about it, but, beyond the initial shock, Sandra's death meant nothing to her. And what, after all, could Julia tell her? Could she show her the note? But that would mean saying more, turning Polly against the father she loved.

Julia emptied her glass, poured herself another. Try seeing it from Polly's point of view. Mother accuses father of affair with younger woman so she herself can go off with younger lover, leaving daughter to as good as kill the father. Aeschylus? Euripides? Clytemnestra? Medea? No, for the moment at least, before Martin's return, she would have to keep her suspicions, her uncertainty, to herself. Or nearly to herself.

Julia picked up her phone.

Almost immediately, Trudy answered. 'Hi, Julia.'

'I'm fine,' Julia said, before realising that she hadn't been asked about her state of health. 'I was wondering whether you were free this coming Wednesday?'

'Wednesday?'

'It's my day off. No teaching duties.' Then, as Trudy didn't reply, she added, 'Sorry, I realise there's not much chance, but if you *do* happen to have an hour or two available I could come to London to see you. Take a train, I mean. It's my turn to visit.'

Trudy said, 'So it is. Wednesday, you say? The morning's out, I'm afraid, but I can manage to escape James's clutches for most of the afternoon.' There was a pause. 'Tell you what. You come in to St Pancras, don't you? Well, then, let's say we meet at Carluccio's, you know where it is? All-purpose Italian food, on the upper floor, under that dreadful statue.'

Julia laughed, her mood lightened by the sound of Trudy's voice, its buoyant warmth.

'I know exactly what you mean,' she said. 'The expense of money in a waste of bronze.'

'That sounds dangerously like poetry,' Trudy said. 'One o'clock Wednesday. Agreed?'

'Agreed,' Julia said. 'I can hob ... hobble that far.'

'Hobble? Julia, are you alright?'

'A figure of speech,' Julia said, and switched the phone off.

Sitting in the encroaching dark, she thought, I should have told Trudy about my accident. And I should have phoned earlier in the evening before I stumbled over my words. I'm drinking too much.

20

'WHAT ON EARTH'S HAPPENED TO YOU?'

As Julia, balancing coffee cup in one hand while she managed her stick in the other, limped over to join Graham, he shook his head in mock sympathy. 'Don't tell me. You've been savaged by a student. Alistair Grenfell?'

Julia lowered herself onto a staff-room chair across the low table from where Graham sat. For an art teacher Graham always looked disconcertingly tidy. No paint-splattered clothes, no wilderness of beard, no suggestion of bohemian excess about his neat jacket and pressed trousers. When, some years before, she'd accused him of letting down the image of art, he'd said, with a dismissive wave of the hand, 'That's *so* last century, darling. Besides, Ronald would never let me out of the house if I wasn't properly attired. He'd be straight round to his lawyer to institute divorce proceedings.'

Julia laughed. 'Not having knife-edge creases is hardly grounds for divorce. Anyway, you're not married.'

But not long afterwards they were. She and Martin had been among the wedding guests who waved them off on a weekend honeymoon in Blackpool, from where they returned with sticks of rock for all and sundry. 'No cliché left unturned,' as Graham said, handing her one. Now, in reply to her having explained about her tumble from the taxi taking her home from Friday night's party, and going so far as to mention Tony Rayburn's ministrations, he said, 'Well, my love, you *were* shall we say a bit squiffy when you left', and made a rocking motion with his hand.

'*Was* I?'

Graham's words upset her. *Had* she been drunk? Was that why she had fallen from the taxi? She felt sudden shame. A saying from her childhood came to her, one an aged aunt often used when rebuking her niece for behaviour likely to be noticed by others. 'Don't make an exhibition of yourself.' She looked at Graham, both hands to her lips, her consternation causing him to laugh.

'Relax, as I imagine Martin has by now learnt to say,' he told her. 'Being drink-taken once in a while isn't a crime against humanity.'

Grimacing, Julia drank her coffee.

Graham nodded sympathetically. 'I quite agree. This coffee *is* a crime, not perhaps a hanging offence, but still ... '

Seeing that nobody had as yet come to join them in the staff-room, Julia, leaning across the table, said, 'Graham, I'm sorry. I'd no idea I was drunk. I'd had a glass or two more than usual, but ... but I didn't do anything awful, did I?'

Graham reached out, took her hand. 'Dear Julia,' he said, 'no, you didn't. Although ... '

She waited for him to continue, and when he remained silent, she asked, 'Although what? What aren't you telling me?'

'It was Ronnie who noticed, not me,' Graham said. Again, he had to be prompted to continue. 'Oh, nothing much. Ronnie wondered whether you and our new member of staff were a little ... a little *cosy*, cosy and clinging, as the song has it.'

'*Tony!* Tony Rayburn?'

'Speak of the devil,' Graham, finger to lips, said, *sotto voce.*

She swung round in her chair. Tony, some twenty or so feet away, raised a hand to them both. He hadn't heard, she was certain of that. But as he came over and, after an embarrassed reply to his question – 'Yes, yes, thanks, much better' – she stood and, stick or no stick, was out of the room in a trice.

***

As she walked away from the college at the end of afternoon classes, Graham on one side of her, Andy Jenkins on the other, the latter said, 'I recommend an office drink for that ankle. Do you the world of good.'

'No,' Julia said firmly, 'I'm on the wagon.'

'An orange juice won't harm you. And we have important matters to discuss.'

The three of them stood at the kerbside as homeward traffic flickered past them. The weather had at last broken, rain had fallen during the night, and now, under cloudy skies and persistent drizzle, the streets were damp and cheerless.

'What matters might those be?' Julia asked. She hunched her shoulders against the wind slapping her face, wished she'd thought to carry a coat before she'd left home, wanted to be back there, making a warm drink, preparing an evening meal, came to the realisation that before she could eat anything she would need to shop. The last of the loaf had gone into the toaster that morning, Polly had scrambled all the eggs for Sunday breakfast – and what else was there, apart from some tinned food, the thought of which revolted her. She had last shopped on the day before the launch party and, as her mother would have said, she was now as good as out of house and home. No cheese, no vegetables, not even an apple. 'I need to get to the supermarket before it closes,' she said to the two men.

Graham took her free arm. 'That gives you plenty of time,' he said, preparing to help her across the road.

Julia looked imploringly at him, saw his answering look. He tugged lightly on her elbow. 'We won't keep you, Julia, I promise. But Andy's right. There are matters to discuss.' And, guiding her as though she was a blind person, he steered her towards the Royal Oak.

Inside, half a dozen other members of staff were grouped round a large table, Tony among them, but when he stood to make room for her she deliberately chose a seat as far away from him as possible.

Andy brought pints for Graham and himself and, for Julia, a glass of sparkling water. Taking a deep mouthful of beer before sitting, he

147

said, as he hooked out a stool for himself, 'I guess we're quorate, in view of which I call the meeting to order. One item for discussion. I'll begin.'

* * *

Some considerable time later, as she stood at her stove, propped on her stick and with her free hand stirring the dubious green and yallery contents of the packet soup she'd bought, together with a wedge of cheddar, fruit, and bagels – the only bread still unsold when she got to the mini-market was the kind of white, sliced loaf which, as Martin once said, ought to have come complete with perforation in order to find its rightful place in the lavatory – she thought with a measure of exasperation about the hour she'd wasted in the Royal Oak listening to Graham and the others blather on about college matters as though they were discussing the fate of nations. 'There are matters to discuss.' Meaning, 'Let's justify sinking a couple of pints by pretending that we care about the insubordination of certain students – aka Grenfell – the exhausting demands of bureaucracy – aka Rudkin's bits of paper – the college's damaging hierarchical structure and its effect on staff morale – aka Janine – and the beneficial, corrective effects of informal, round-table, discussions – aka "It's Your Round" – followed at last by AOB – aka "Good god, is that the time, I must fly."'

At least Tony had kept his thoughts to himself. Once or twice she'd noticed him glancing at his watch, and she thought she'd detected a degree of impatience in the way he answered Andy's needling invitation to share with the others his impressions of teaching colleagues – 'Are they up to standard?' brought the response 'Why shouldn't they be?' – but for the most part he sat silent until, patience presumably exhausted, he stood, said a general goodbye and left.

His going was the excuse for Julia, too, to leave. As she got to her feet she noticed the raised eyebrow which accompanied the glance Andy directed at Graham, and irritation flared, became momentary resentment, a stab of anger. But she exited without saying anything.

Outside, she stood for a moment watching cars as, lights on, they moved through the early dusk, then she turned and limped the few yards to where Tony stood at the bus stop. 'How are you feeling?' he asked, glancing at her strapped ankle. It was the same question that he had asked that morning, and from the awkward way he spoke she realised that he was ill-at-ease.

'Better,' Julia said. 'Thank you.' After a moment, she added, 'I ought to have dropped you a note to say how grateful I was for your help.' She offered him a wry smile. 'But of course I didn't have your address.' The words sounded stiff, formal, ungracious. And, conscious of how she'd seated herself well away from him in the pub, she added, as though by way of acknowledging the shame which Graham's words earlier in the day had occasioned, 'I think I must have drunk more than was good for me.'

'You were fine,' Tony said. 'That accident, it wasn't your fault – it could have happened to anyone.'

No, she wanted to tell him, it couldn't. I *had* drunk too much and as everyone knows, you should never drink when you're depressed. But instead, and in an attempt to deflect her thoughts, she decided to apologise for the previous, wasted hour in the Oak. 'I could see you were anxious to get away from that so-called meeting.'

'Ah, well,' Tony said, shrugging. 'It might have been important.'

But Julia was determined to atone. 'I'd say that was very unlikely.' And when he looked enquiringly at her, she said, 'When women meet – for a coffee or over a cup of tea – they make no bones about the fact that they enjoy the chance for what's called "small talk". And I bet it wasn't a woman who came up with *that* phrase.' She waited for Tony to acknowledge her words, then went on, 'Men claim that having a drink is an excuse for important discussions. What used to be called a Big Production. But it's the other way round, isn't it? Talk, often very small talk, is the excuse for drink. Downing a beer, isn't it called? Downing several is more like it.'

Tony laughed. 'Got us bang to rights,' he said.

'Still,' Julia said, feeling rather better about herself, 'I exonerate you. It was *me* who had too much to drink last Friday and this evening it was *you* who wanted to leave the others to their drink.'

'I have an article to finish,' he said. 'And here's the bus.'

She looked to where he was pointing, saw the double-decker in the far distance lumbering towards where they stood.

They took seats near the front. 'I need to get off before my usual stop,' Julia explained. 'I have to re-stock the larder.' But as she rang the bell and hauled herself upright she refused his offer of further help. 'Thanks, Tony, but I'd rather manage on my own. Hasten the recovery. I need to be fighting fit for the weekend.'

I wish I hadn't said that, she thought, as she stood at the kerbside and watched the bus as it disappeared round a corner of the road taking Tony Rayburn away from her.

***

Sitting at the kitchen table, she spooned in a mouthful of soup, swallowed with reluctance, then pushed the bowl away from her. Reaching for her phone, she read Martin's most recent text message. It had been sent earlier that day, ten o'clock at night by his time. *May Day Reminder Plane arrives Heathrow at 11 am Sat. Should be home by mid-afternoon. No need for bunting, brass band optional. Jet-lag probable, sleep needed. Then raring to go and fighting fit. Mx*

After a moment's hesitation, Julia texted back. *Message recd and understood. Me too fighting fit. J*

Let him make of that what he will, she thought.

21

TUESDAY EVENING. A BETTER MEAL THAN last night's. I made myself a mushroom omelette with salad and a glass of water. No wine! While I ate I listened to a favourite CD: *Franck's Orchestral Variations and Violin Sonata*, and indulged myself remembering early adolescent years when I still dreamed of becoming an orchestral violinist. And now I can't even remember when I last took the instrument out of its case. Perhaps guilt – or envy – explains why I threw a five-pound note into the hat of the young man busking outside the supermarket where I shopped on the way home from college. I could hear his solo violin playing rapid Gypsy tunes à la Grappelli that came filtering through the store doors as I stocked up with necessaries, and even found myself thinking about what I might buy for the weekend until I came to and told myself I had no intention of killing the fatted calf against M's return. Though goodness knows what will happen. I'll need to decide how to confront him with what occurred between him and the girl. And exactly *when* do I tell him that I know? Presumably when he gets in he'll want – need – to crash out for a few hours. I ought to discuss this with Trudy when we meet tomorrow. And suppose he wants me to meet him at the station? What do I say? My ankle won't let me ... I haven't of course told him about Graham and Ronnie's party and he knows nothing about Tony Rayburn. Not that there's anything to know. But I did something silly today, another matter I shall have to discus with Trudy.

I managed to keep out of Tony's way for most of the day but then, as I was leaving college, he appeared in the foyer, and we walked together to the edge of campus. He wasn't going home, he told me, wouldn't be walking any further with me. Instead, he was heading towards the town centre's public library. Some references he needed to check before he could send his article to the journal which had already seen and approved the abstract he'd sent them. He was quite excited about the prospect of appearing in this particular journal, one even I had heard of, because, as M, who appears there regularly more than once has told me, it's a leader in the field, a maker of reputations. Tony, I assume, has hopes of getting a proper academic post rather than seeing out time in a college of FE. I can't blame him for that. Ambition is no bad thing, and, though I didn't say that to him, I did go so far as to say I hoped he'd be suitably rewarded for his work. A bit pompous, but he made the right kind of answer: murmured that work was its own reward, that he'd learnt as a student the true meaning of disinterested research – and, yes, I said, I couldn't bear hearing people use the word when they simply meant 'uninterested'.

Tony laughed at my show of irritation, which in fact is genuine because I can't stand the misuse of the word; he said he rather feared the town library might prove to be uninterested in his specialism. 'God knows if they can supply the references I need.' And that was when I made an offer I now regret. If the library couldn't come up trumps, I told him, he'd be welcome to try my husband's library, see whether that contained what he needed.

'Oh, *could* I?' He was all gratitude and at once I felt I shouldn't have made the invitation. It's a reasonable guess that Martin has somewhere on his shelves the reference books Tony is after, but I don't know that I should have offered him the run of the study, not when M is away. Besides which ...

Perhaps he saw that I wasn't entirely at ease with my own proposal because he said that he was probably being unfair to the public library, which was after all quite a sizeable one, and you never knew ... He'd let me know tomorrow how he'd got on.

Not tomorrow, I told him, I'll be in London – Wednesday's my free day. But I'll be back in college on Thursday. So we agreed that he'd let me know then whether, if my offer still held, he'd want to take it up. I had the impression we both felt somehow ill-at-ease, as if my offer and his acceptance made for a solecism we couldn't handle. At all events, he turned pretty abruptly from me and I watched him march briskly up the street in the direction of the city centre before, trying not to limp, I made for my bus stop.

As I did so I saw Graham and Andy come sauntering down the college drive. No prizes for guessing where they were off to. They waved to me and I waved back. Presumably they'd seen Tony and me in conversation but I had no intention of waiting to find out, let alone of joining them in the Oak, so I shouted out that I was off to do some shopping and walked away.

Break. The Franck having come to an end I placed the CD back in its case and as I did so noticed lying near it that Vaughan Williams – *The Norfolk Rhapsodies, Fantasia on Tallis, Lark Ascending* – the CD Polly always chose when the three of us had breakfast together on a Saturday. Our family routine. Stewed fruit, scrambled egg, which, as she grew older she took such pride in making for us all, careful to follow exactly the additional flavouring we'd evolved – a pinch of dry mustard, half a teaspoon of tarragon – toast, and for M and me, coffee we drank from cups we'd bought in a French market soon after we were married, milky tea for our daughter. We were blithely breakfasting all, weren't we? Ah no, the years, the years. Damn. Damn. Damn.

Julia sat staring at the page she'd just written. I hate this damp nostalgia, she thought. Polly is happy, in love, looking forward to a new life. Rejoice for her.

And Martin and I?

She got up from her chair. I must lay out my clothes for tomorrow. Then a bath and early to bed. I have a day in London to look forward to, meeting my recently-acquired friend, Trudy. Odd, that, how close she felt to a woman she'd met on holiday but who had become so much more than a holiday friend. But then she, Julia, had, she acknowledged, few friends of her own. Acquaintances, yes, but from her student years it had somehow been accepted that Martin's friends were hers, too, and should suffice. And then, with the birth of Polly, she had been absorbed in her daughter and Polly's shifting and re-forming circles of girlhood friends. She had never felt the need for close relationships apart from those her family provided. But now her parents were dead, Polly was leaving for America, and Martin ...

STOP IT!

Shocked by the sound of her own voice, its cry of angry protest, she looked guiltily round. But nobody could hear. Nobody was there.

22

TRUDY WAS WAITING FOR HER AT the ticket barrier.

Julia limped towards her, and after they'd embraced, Trudy stood back to examine her friend, her smile part-quizzical, part-concerned. 'What happened?' she asked. 'I'd been thinking we might give Carluccio's a miss, go somewhere more interesting, but now I'm not so sure.' She looked down at the bandaged ankle that showed below Julia's jeans, took in the walking stick, raised her eyes to meet her friend's, and said, 'You won't get far on one leg.'

Julia waited until the crush of fellow passengers leaving the concourse had lessened before, laughing, she said, 'Don't you believe it. I've got to London, haven't I?'

'Not by walking, you haven't.' And as she began to lead the way to the escalator that would take them down to the station's vast, ground-level concourse, Trudy, standing beside her friend, arm locked into hers, repeated her question. 'What happened?'

'I tripped – getting out of a taxi.'

Trudy gave Julia's arm a squeeze. 'Pissed?'

'I suppose I must have been. Anyway, I'm over the worst.'

As they stepped off the escalator and began the slow manoeuvre between clusters of people, many of them with large wheelie cases, others forcing their way towards coffee-bars and dress-shops with which the concourse was lined – 'Just like bloody Heathrow,' Trudy shouted above the hubbub. 'Empty your pockets, dear people, before you even get to your destination' – Julia, having paused to listen to an

154

inexpert pianist's version of 'Ain't Misbehavin'', a number her father had once liked to play and sing – shouted back, 'Where were you planning to take me?'

'It's not far,' Trudy said, leaning to speak into her friend's ear. 'Can you manage a fifteen-minute walk?'

'Of course I can. And after an hour and a half on a crowded train the fresh air will do me good.'

'I hope you brought your own,' Trudy said, as they made for the exit onto the Euston Road. 'You won't find any in London.'

The pub restaurant, off Gray's Inn Road, was surprisingly quiet. As they settled themselves at the table Trudy had reserved, she leant across to Julia and in a mock whisper asked her, 'First impressions, please?'

Julia looked around, took in the long bar, the tables where men and women, most of them in suits, were deep in conversation, though one or two prodded at smart phones, and said, 'No laptops.'

'Very good,' Trudy said. 'They're banned. Anything else?'

Julia looked again then back at her friend, took in Trudy's high-necked, navy blue blouse, maroon jacket, and said, 'You're looking lovely.'

'So are you,' Trudy said, 'Pale green suits you, but that's not what I mean.'

And when Julia looked enquiringly at her, she said, 'No music. That's banned, too. Here, we can talk without having to shout.' She laughed, delightedly. 'And the food's not bad, either.'

Which it wasn't. Julia chose grilled sole, her friend had a plate of glistening, yellow tagliatelle, and they shared a half bottle of Orvieto. 'Unspectacular but serviceable,' Trudy said after an initial sip, her voice a ripe imitation of wine-snobbism. She put down her glass. 'Now,' she said, 'before you tell me what's on your mind, let me tell you that last evening James and I had a visit from Giles. He's in town for some conference or other and took the chance to drop in for a chat and to let us know how well his lectures were received in San Francisco. Apparently the natives were beside themselves with wonder. Even Orlando was impressed, so we were assured.' She forked up a piece of tagliatelle. 'I'd quite like to hear Orlando's version of that, wouldn't you?'

Julia fiddled with her fork. 'Did he have anything to say about Martin?' She looked up, saw Trudy's eyes were on her, and looked away.

'As a matter of fact he did,' Trudy said. 'There was the to-be-expected stuff about Professor Gibbs's talks and general contribution to the intellectual life of the institution being much appreciated – almost as much as Giles's, James and I were no doubt meant to infer – but I doubt that's what will interest you.' She lifted her glass, drank, returned it to the white-clothed table, and said, 'Giles worried from one or two remarks Martin let drop that all might not be well between you two. There now. Either he's become unusually observant or Martin ... ' She chose not to finish the sentence.

Julia did then meet her friend's steady gaze. 'I don't know how he could gain that impression. I've said nothing.'

Trudy nodded, said, 'Perhaps that's why Martin is, to use Giles's word, worried. According to Giles, you haven't always answered your husband's calls or messages, and when you have, you've been – again according to Giles – "brief and to the point."'

Julia laid aside her fork. 'It's true,' she said, 'that I don't like using any kind of messaging service. I never know what to say. But Martin knows that.' She stared at her plate, said quietly, 'But it's also true that I don't know what to say to him.' She raised her eyes. 'What *can* I say until I see him face to face?' She picked up her fork. 'Then I'll have plenty to say.' She swallowed a sliver of fish. If I'm still there, that is. But she didn't say that. Instead, laying aside her fork, she said, 'And in the meantime I have another explanation for Giles's concern.'

'Which is why you're here.'

'Yes, to be honest it is, though I hoped you wouldn't mind.'

'I don't,' Trudy said. 'It's what friends are for, and who knows, next time I may need your shoulder to cry on.'

'Oh, Trudy.' Julia waited for a couple newly arrived at the next table to settle themselves before she said, 'Is anything wrong between you and James?'

Shaking her head, Trudy laughed as she said, 'Not a thing. A bed of roses, a bowl of cherries, a ... well, I can't think of any other clichés, but we're fine. I was speaking hypothetically.' She drained her glass, shared the rest of the wine between them, and pointing the emptied bottle at Julia, ordered, 'Now, as the medicine man would say, tell me what's eating you.'

Which Julia did.

By the time she'd finished their plates had been cleared and coffees placed in front of them.

For some moments Trudy sat, forehead creased, staring at her cappuccino. Then, slowly, she said, 'So you think Giles was helping Martin out by offering to take this Sandra off his hands, and his trip to San Francisco was by way of claiming a belated reward?'

'Don't you?' Julia asked. 'Martin told me Giles wouldn't be going.'

Trudy sighed. 'I'll tell you what I *do* think, that if all this is true then it's pretty squalid.'

'I agree,' Julia said. 'And how am I supposed to raise the subject – until Martin's back home? And before then, I can't discuss it with Polly. She adores her father.'

'And might, who knows, take his side?'

The question was like a sword thrust. She's guessed why I daren't speak to Polly, Julia thought miserably. But she said nothing.

'Martin will be back soon, won't he?'

Averting her eyes, Julia said, 'Saturday. I'm *dreading* it.'

In the ensuing silence, Trudy raised a hand to attract the waiter's attention.

'Let me, please.' Julia put a hand on her friend's arm. 'I'm visiting all my cares on you, it's the least repayment I can make.'

'It was going to be my treat,' Trudy said. 'But if you insist ... '

As they waited for the bill to arrive, Trudy said, 'Tell me about this Tony Rayburn.'

'Oh,' Julia said, 'I thought I had. Mid-thirties, I guess, one marriage been and gone, ambitious to become an academic success, though not pushy, tall, reasonably good looking ... '

'He sounds a good bargain for some aspiring lady. Or is he gay?'

The waiter hovered as Julia paid by card, glanced at the amount she'd entered, said a gracious 'Thank you, madam', and with a flourish tore off and gave her the receipt together with her card. 'Have a nice day,' he said, as he turned away.

'Gay?' Julia stood, tucked her wallet into her shoulder bag. 'No, he's been married. I said.'

Trudy, also standing, said, 'He wouldn't be the first to walk out of a marriage because he preferred men.'

'I don't think he's one of them.'

'Oh?' But Trudy's smile was no more than a gentle, quizzical enquiry.

As they came, after their slow, dragging walk, to the top of the stairs leading to the underground – Trudy was taking the Northern Line to Camden Town – Julia said, turning to face her friend, 'Reason proves Love deceives at every turn. Unquote. Remember?' Then, kissing her on the cheek, she added, 'But I'm more grateful than I can say for the chance to talk.'

'It was nothing,' Trudy said, as crowds of men and women jostled and swarmed about them. Then, into Julia's ear, she said, 'I mean I'm glad if I was of use. Sorority. Remember?'

'You were, and I do,' Julia said, letting go of Trudy's arm.

And a few minutes later she was on her train, once more jolting her way through the home counties and into the Midlands, back to where she lived, back to her home.

23

'LOOK AT THIS.' TONY, DROPPING INTO a chair beside Julia, put a piece of paper in front of her as she sat drinking coffee in the staff-room. The paper bore the college crest and below it, in bold lettering FROM THE DESK OF DAVID RUDKIN, BA, CERT. MS, COLLEGE SECRETARY.

> Payroll and finance partnership. New arrangements. Delivering a new invoice scanning solution. This is an important and exciting move forward as we embrace developments in technology to implement an Optical Character Recognition system which extracts information directly from an invoice and pre-populates the details into our accounting system. This will support us in providing a more efficient and effective service to our customers.

By the time Julia had read and re-read this missive and with a shrug of mock despair given up any attempt to find a way through the thickets of Rudkin's impenetrable prose, she and Tony had been joined by several other members of staff, Graham among them. All, it seemed, had found Rudkin's message waiting for them in their pigeon-holes.

'Has anyone *any* idea what he means?' Andy asked, looking round the table. Someone, not Graham, said, 'We'd need a long meeting at the Oak to answer that question.'

'Life's too short,' Andy said. 'It's what comes of letting admin wear new suits. As a result, you'll have noticed that we're no longer staff members. We're customers and they're selling us short.' He stabbed at the top of the paper with an index finger. 'Cert. MS. What's it mean? My guess is Certifiable Mad Sod.'

Graham said, 'He hasn't got that painted on his door. Perhaps he's just bought it.'

'Mail Order,' Andy said. 'From *Bespoke Degrees, Bangalore.*'

Tony said, 'It's Rudkin's way of telling us what we already know. Translated into English it means that if we want to buy a piece of equipment for teaching purposes we need to present an invoice or we won't get our money back.'

'Well, that lets me out,' Julia said. 'Part-timers aren't allowed to buy in any teaching aid. We have to request the college to buy for us. And the request is usually refused. We can't even ask for books to be bought in by the library.'

Andy grinned evilly at her. 'Not a proper customer,' he said.

Julia stood. 'No,' she said, suddenly angry. 'We're not.'

'Something tells me you're not best pleased with life,' Andy said.

'Andy, your powers of deduction never cease to amaze me,' Julia said, still angry. 'When I got in this morning,' she told him and the others, 'I found a note from Rudkin asking me to "fill-in" as he graciously put it, for two classes tomorrow. Apparently the Head of English is off at some day conference "representing the college's best interests." But classes must go ahead as normal. We can't have the students complaining. So I have to jump to it. Naturally there was no mention of extra money. So I shan't be required to ... what is it?' She leant over Tony's shoulder. 'To implement an Optical Character Recognition.'

She gathered up her books, said to Tony, 'I'll see you later, Tony', letting the others make of her remark what they would, and left.

***

Later meant that evening. The previous afternoon, on the train back from London, she found two messages on the phone she'd switched off while she and Trudy were together. The first was from Martin. It had been sent one a.m. his time and was brief and to the point. *Just back from dinner following my last lecture. Now for a few hours sleep before I head*

for the airport. Next stop New Jersey, then Heathrow, then home Mx.
Re-reading the terse message she became certain there was something
evasive about it. What had Trudy told her of Giles's suspicions?
Perhaps, though, now she thought of it, there was something odd in the
fact that Martin had made few attempts to phone her, as if – could it be?
– he wanted for some reason to avoid the risk of conversation, had no
intention of talking to her from San Francisco, of having to ... to what?
Explain about the note that – who knows? – it occurred to him she might
by chance have stumbled on. Well, she'd soon enough find out.

Should she reply? She sent him the briefest of replies. *Bon voyage.*
Then she erased it and turned to the other message.

It was from Tony. *Is the kind offer for me to consult your husband's
library still open? If so, I'd like to take you up on it. As expected the town
library didn't have the books I needed. Tomorrow evening perhaps?*

To this, Julia texted back: *Yes, of course. Come to supper. 7 pm.*

And now, at a little after seven o'clock, there was a knock on the front
door, and Tony loomed in the porch. Julia stood aside to let him in and
before closing the door looked towards her neighbour's garden, though
in the deepening dusk Muriel Dawson's hedge was no more than a
blurred outline and anyway the thought she might be lurking behind it
was pleasantly absurd.

Julia led the way into the kitchen where Tony, having handed over a
bottle of wine he produced from his shoulder bag, stood awkwardly
fingering the zip of his rain jacket. She sensed that he was embarrassed,
was remembering the occasion of his previous visit and unsure whether
to mention it. 'Give me your coat,' she said briskly, 'and do sit', and she
gestured to the table where she'd laid two places and a large bowl of
green salad. 'Will this do? I've not had time for much shopping, I'm
afraid.' She could hardly say that she'd spent a long hour in front of her
bedroom mirror, trying on various outfits, before, and with some
hesitation, finally deciding on an old pair of jeans and blue sweater, set
off by a red, knotted, neck scarf. 'You'll do,' she said to her reflection,
though with no enthusiasm. The shadows under her eyes were deeper
and darker than she could bear to study for more than a moment. Not
old, maybe, she said, but not renewable, either. And as she thought that,

she remembered the young woman whose eyes had met hers in the shared mirror of The Fisherman's Rest on the evening of Graham and Ronnie's launching party. 'Good luck,' the woman, scarcely out of her teenage years, had said then. 'Good luck,' Julia now said to herself, but without allowing herself to consider what she might mean. Then she clumped downstairs.

Now, handing him a slice of quiche, she saw that his dark grey jacket was new, and that his open-neck, blue-check shirt, was at least freshly ironed.

'This is perfect,' he said, picking up his fork then laying it down so that it chinked faintly against his plate. He seemed as nervous as she felt. 'I don't want to put you to any trouble.'

As if on cue, Julia stood abruptly. 'I forgot glasses,' she said, and went to fetch them. 'You pour,' she ordered, as she placed the glasses in front of both of them, and resumed her seat. 'But only a very little for me.'

Then, realising her words were responsible for his quick, slightly guilty look, she added, 'I'm still doing penance for last Friday.'

'But you're walking more easily.' The words sounded as if he needed reassurance that he wasn't to blame for her accident.

'Yes,' she said, reaching for her half-filled glass, and allowing herself an experimental sip. 'Come Saturday I'll be as fit as a flea.'

He smiled at that. 'My grandmother used to say "fit as a pudding". I once asked her why a pudding should be fit and she said "So it can fill a small boy's stomach". She was a reet champion pudding-maker.' He smirked as he tried out the fake northern voice.

Julia pushed the salad bowl towards him. 'Did you have a favourite pudding?'

'Steak and kidney,' he said. 'She could have won a gold medal with hers.'

Before Julia could stop herself, she said, 'One of my husband's favourite meals.'

'If my gran was still with us I'd ask her to make him one,' Tony said. Then, 'He's due back soon?'

She nodded. 'Saturday.'

'You must be looking forward to seeing him again.' Tony raised his glass. 'Should we wish him a safe journey?' But he stopped, put down his glass, said with a slight shake of the head, a self-rebuke. 'Better not. My gran always used to say it brought bad luck.'

Julia said firmly, 'In that case let's not make a wish.'

'No,' he said, contrite. 'That was stupid. I'm sorry.'

To break the awkward pause, Julia said, 'Do you remember many of your grandmother's sayings?'

'Quite a few. I was round at her house a lot when I was growing up. After my father left – went off with someone else – my mother took full-time work so I used to have my supper at gran's. She fed me up.'

'And you were soon as fat as a pudding.'

He laughed at that. 'No,' he said, 'she told me I was one of Jacob's lean kind. At least I thought that was the word. But then I found out she was saying "kine".' He looked at Julia, smiled ruefully, before adding, 'I don't suppose anyone uses that nowadays.'

'I don't suppose they do,' Julia said.

She drank a little more of her wine, picked at her food, noticed that Tony was eating quickly. Hungry? Wanting to get the meal done with so he could do what he'd come for and get away?

'I'm sorry I can't offer you any more,' Julia said.

He looked at his empty plate, then at her, smiled apologetically. 'I'm a greedy feeder,' he said.

'Another of your gran's sayings?'

He shook his head. 'My own.' He emptied his glass, lifted the bottle and looked enquiringly at Julia.

'You go ahead,' she told him, 'I'll pass. But I could make coffee if you'd like.'

In the act of pouring more wine, he paused, said, 'Good idea. Keep me sober for the task ahead.'

Over coffee they talked, briefly, about life at college. She voiced her irritation at the way part-timers were so often ignored by administration over college matters – 'We're always the last to know. Even the students get more information about what people like Rudkin call "College Developments".'

Perhaps prompted by her words, Tony wanted to hear more about

Janine Hamilton. Was she a good Principal? Did she do her best to look after her staff, or was she at the beck and call of Administration? Julia said she thought that Janine was becoming increasingly semi-detached from the place. 'Her husband's a wealthy man and she may be planning to leave sometime soon. Anyway, that's the rumour.'

Tony nodded. 'It figures. I went to see her the other day, to suggest a few changes to the way History's taught. She didn't seem interested. Told me no changes would be possible until next summer and by then who could tell what might be happening? I got the impression she neither knew nor cared.'

He leant back in his chair, smiled as if taking for granted her understanding of the frustration his words, mild though they were, implied, and Julia sensed that the mood between them was becoming more relaxed, the earlier stiffness gone now. Two professionals together, that's what they were, their grousing over college life the means to create an atmosphere they could jointly breathe, a warmth into which they could both lean. A further half hour during which they emptied the coffee jug and Julia, knowing her words wouldn't be misunderstood, could stand, could even laugh, as she remarked, 'Time, I think, to take you upstairs.'

And as she showed him into her husband's study, she was able to tell him, smiling, that when he'd found and checked the references he needed, she'd be waiting for him downstairs.

***

It was only after he'd left that Julia could admit to herself that her half-formed thought – no, not even that – that the vaporous fancy which her invitation to him had set off became, as the evening progressed, such stuff as dreams are made on. Could she have forced the issue? Not really. She could imagine Trudy, supposing Julia had consulted her, urging her to seize the chance, to go for it, to drag Tony into bed if need be. But Trudy would have been laughing as she offered her advice. And it was laughable, though in a way, she realised, Trudy wouldn't have understood. Even if Tony had entertained – was that the word? – the

164

possibility of going to bed with her, Julia would had havered as she had in front of a mirror before deciding what to wear. Passion hadn't so much died as failed to come to life as they sat facing each other over quiche and salad. There had been no missed opportunity. There had been nothing, nothing between them but a gradual thawing into friendly regard.

So why wasn't she laughing? Why, on the contrary, did she feel a bleak chill surrounding her, its touch creeping across her skin so that, sitting at her table, she involuntarily shivered? I lack solace, she thought, remembering a line from *Love's Labour's Lost*, a play she had read as an undergraduate and with which, despite the dismissal of its worth by her tutor, she had fallen in love, though puzzled by much, including the order Berowne gives to his fellow courtiers, young men who, having renounced the world, almost at once find themselves in love with a party of young women. 'We will with some strange pastime solace them,' Berowne says. Why on earth should the women need solacing? Solace meant offering consolation in a time of sorrow, surely, and the young women seemed happy enough. But her dictionary set her to rights. In Shakespeare's time the word had also meant to make cheerful, even to entertain, to amuse. A useful lesson, that, and one she was always passing onto her students. Words have histories, over time many of them change their meanings. Always keep a good dictionary to hand so you can look up the meanings of words. She doubted that many of them did and those who did sometimes made spectacular mistakes. There had been the foreign student whose essay on *Tess of the D'Urbervilles* remarked that Alec had seduced the heroine and caused her to become gravid. How difficult it had been to explain to the student that although the word was technically correct nobody any longer used it to mean pregnant. 'But the dictionary so tells,' the poor girl had said, tears in her eyes.

Words, Julia thought, as she climbed into bed, how they can mislead. And trying to sleep, she saw the scrap of paper and the words, '*Martin I can't go on. Tomorrow will be too late.*'

24

LATE ON FRIDAY AFTERNOON JULIA LOST her temper. By now she should have finished her teaching week, but because of Rudkin's directive masquerading as request she was teaching two extra classes of students, none of whom seemed at all interested in the material she had got up extra early that morning to prepare. It wasn't them, however, who sent her into a rage. They, or anyway most of them, made no bones about revealing a bored indifference to the anthology of modern poetry they were supposed to be studying. The more she enthused, the more they yawned, gazed out of the window or at each other, or sneaked looks at watches or the phones they weren't supposed to take into class but did.

She didn't necessarily blame them. They were young, the weekend was coming when, as the poets had it, including poets in the very anthology in which they showed no interest, they could be in one another's arms or stopping by any rainy park to watch folks kick a ball until it's dark or freewheeling down the escarpment past the unpassing horse, or standing at the corner of some bar, or even, church-going, where they'd mutter Here Endeth much more loudly than they'd meant.

At six o'clock she dismissed the last class of the day, stuffed her books into the leather bag bought years ago in a Greek market, and was about to leave when Rudkin appeared in the doorway.

'I had hoped to find you here,' he said. In his suit with white shirt and tightly-knotted tie he was the epitome of petty officialdom.

Julia looked at him enquiringly but said nothing.

'Yes,' Rudkin said, advancing into the room. 'I had hoped to find you here.'

After a moment, during which he had said nothing but fixed on her an unwavering gaze, she asked, 'Why?'

He stood now close enough for her to smell his aftershave or, more likely, the sharp, unpleasant tang of deodorant. His smile emollient, he said, 'We need to ensure that all classes are correctly maintained.'

Julia said, 'What on earth is that supposed to mean?'

'It means,' Rudkin said, still keeping his gaze on her, 'that the Vice-Principal and I have become aware of a degree of irregularity in the keeping of tutor hours.'

Julia was taken aback. 'Are you accusing me of having skipped my teaching duties?'

Then, when he said nothing, she asked, mystified and in the same instant aware of anger throbbing in her veins, flushing her face, 'Has anyone – any student – been complaining about me?'

'About *you*? No, no.' Rudkin held up a hand like a traffic policeman. 'But I believe you are friendly with Dr Rayburn.'

'What of it?'

Rudkin looked round the empty classroom before, lowering his voice, he said, 'I am afraid there have been one or two complaints about his ... methods, shall we say. And the fact that he has from time to time brought classes to an end before the due hour. *And*, we are led to believe, that he has shown an amount of ... of unwise favouritism towards female students in particular.'

'This is Grenfell, isn't it?' Julia said, suddenly wise.

The thin smile on Rudkin's pursed lips was intended to be judicious. 'As you know, it is a college rule that in the first instant any complainant – or complainants – be guaranteed anonymity.'

'So why are you mentioning this to me?'

'I hardly need to spell it out, surely? You are thought to be friendly with Dr Rayburn. I hoped you would be willing to have a word with your ... your friend ... '

'And tell him what? That some shit of a student is planning to knife him in the back?'

Rudkin said nothing, merely looked at her, a sliver of pink tongue appearing between his lips.

'You know,' Julia said, trying to control the rage that made her heart pound, thickened her tongue. 'You know ... '

She stopped, tried again. 'Do I get paid for doing your dirty work for you?' she asked. She drew breath. 'Or is this another chore I'm expected to take on for love of college?' Still, he said nothing, though his smile was now uncertain.

'And by the way' – she was shouting – 'it's not Tony Rayburn who needs to be warned. It's you, you ... '

As she brushed by Rudkin on her way to the door, she heard his words. 'Are you threatening me?'

Wild with anger, she span round but the words she wanted wouldn't come. 'You are *pathetic*,' was all she could manage. And she left, slamming the door behind her.

***

Friday evening. I'm still simmering from the row I had with that pompous toad, Rudkin. I'm not sure why I became so angry, why I didn't laugh in his face at his ludicrous attempt to play the gauleiter. I don't think my rage was unreasonable but even so I'd have done better to keep cool. Rudkin will find a way to get back at me. Well, let him. Anyway, I may soon be wanting to leave town. I suppose I'd better warn Tony about Grenfell, though it can wait until Monday, no need to spoil his weekend. But what did Rudkin mean about me being '*friendly* with Dr Rayburn'? The way he looked at me when he said the word, the stress he laid on it, was presumably his version of nudge, nudge, whispers, a little bird told me ... Lovers, is that what you're hinting? Well, no you fat fraud, we aren't lovers, nor ever will be, as last evening made abundantly clear. We're good friends, no more, no less.

Even so I may as well admit within the confines of these pages that at first I was, I know I was, hoping for more, though I've no idea how I'd have responded if Tony had made advances. Would I have grabbed him, hauled him into bed? But he didn't, did he? And I didn't want him to. There, that's the truth, Mr Bloody Rudkin.

But here's a further admission. Dear Diary, Dear Journal, I'm *lonely*. Trudy is becoming a close friend but there are limits to what I can tell her. And dear, dear Polly – how can I talk to her about Martin? Though, of course, if I *do* leave him she'll have to be told why. And for all that I feel such anger at him – an anger which, now I think of it, must have spilled over when Rudkin confronted me with his stupid request – I don't want to turn Polly against her father. I'm not, am I, a vindictive woman? And suppose she takes his side ... ?

Julia straightened up, looked round the kitchen, wanting to be comforted by familiar sights: the washing-machine with its Cyclops's eye wedged next to the fridge, draining board supporting the single – ha! – cup and plate she'd painstakingly washed after her evening meal of cold ham and salad, the calendar pinned to the wall beside the blue-curtained window, ringing, she knew tomorrow's date, the date of Martin's return ...

Deep breath, now, as we pass quickly on to the outer door, its hook from which dangled shopping bags and an old mac ... Now, Julia, why don't I close my eyes and play the memory tray game? A perfect game for a woman on her own.

Abruptly, she stood, threw down her pen, and went into the front room. There, dropped onto the sofa where Tony had made up a bed for her on the night of her accident. I could play the game equally well here, she thought. Even though, that night apart, I've hardly used the room since Martin's departure, I know the shape and colour of each chair, the position of the TV, the paintings ... and then there's the back room – my study – where I keep my books and the desk I brought from my own teenage bedroom and which houses my computer with the filing cabinet beside it, and photographs of Polly – Polly on her own or with Martin and me, and now with Al – and cards celebrating special occasions propped on so many surfaces ... I can remember when and where most of the articles were bought, and why: sometimes on a whim, sometimes because one of us fell in love with them, or to keep fresh the memory of a place or an event where we were happy, the pictures and the cutlery, the tinkling piano in the next apartment. The music in the piano stool. That vase ...

A wave of emotion travelled up from the soles of her feet: she trembled, felt it gripping her throat, it filled her eyes. 'This is my home,' she said aloud, when she could speak, 'Nobody is allowed to take it away from me. *Nobody.*'

The phone in the kitchen rang and as well as her still sore ankle allowed she hastened through to take the call.

'Mum,' Polly's voice said. 'I thought I'd phone now because tomorrow you'll want to be alone with Dad when he gets in, so I'll phone again on Sunday. But give him all my love. And Al sends love to you both. Bye.' And without waiting for Julia to say anything she rang off.

And above all, Julia thought, replacing the receiver, above all I don't want to lose Polly.

V

25

THE RING TONE WOKE HER.

Still bleary from the sleep she had at last managed to fall into, Julia listened as, voice sounding strained, perhaps from fatigue, Martin told her that the queue at passport control would probably take at least another hour to get through, after which there would be the journey to St Pancras, then a wait for the train he was hoping to catch, but that, assuming he took a taxi from the station, with luck he'd be home in five hours, six at the latest. 'I'll call from the train,' he said, 'let you know when you can expect me.'

'Yes,' she said, 'please do', and switched off.

She lay back, heart thumping under her ribs as if she'd just run up two flights of stairs, on her back a laden rucksack. That old exercise! A student friend had recommended it to Julia when she admitted to worrying over what she later realised was a non-existent weight problem. She could hear it now, Martin's laugh of disbelief when she confessed her worry, his passionate insistence on her body's perfection, at least as far as he was concerned, and who else's concern could her body possibly be, and, in reply to his questioning her about her judgement on his own body, her teasing him about the hairs clustered thickly round his groin. Did he put them in curlers every night? She was pushing her fingers through them as she asked her question, relishing that springy, spiky texture, and he was stroking her breasts, coaxing the nipples into stiffness. How simple love had been, and how complete, making one little room an everywhere. For a few moments Julia drifted in a reverie of the delight she and Martin had found in each other's bodies, the thrilled, and as it seemed, inexhaustible discovery and mapping of new worlds.

No! Stop it.

She sat upright, forced herself from bed.

Half an hour later, showered and breakfasted, she sat at the kitchen table, making a shopping list for the weekend. Beyond that I need not go, she thought, and tried to concentrate on other matters. There were bills to settle, she needed to call at the bank in order to put money in her wallet; and she must find time to run the vacuum over the house, though so little had she varied her month-long occupation of kitchen and bedroom that dusting and cleaning could be done in what her mother would have called two shakes of a lamb's tail.

And then what?

Then I sit and wait for him to walk in.

And *then* what?

Then I show him Sandra's note, pack my bags and walk out?

And *then* what?

Something like panic gripped her bowels. The past month became unreal, a weird, almost fake prologue to the act which, in her repeated attempts to imagine it, always moved towards the same conclusion. There, she was in control. Martin uttered the scripts she devised, he was contrite, abashed, and when in one version he brushed aside her outrage, her vehement cry of betrayal, her guilty verdict on his seduction of a hapless student and its squalid aftermath, her accusation of Giles's collusion and the poor girl's death, he was forced to take refuge in bluster or indifference. There was one version she couldn't or wouldn't devise. Martin humiliating her with a plausible explanation. That belonged in the reject pile of possibilities. No, however the confrontation developed it surely ended with ...

With what? What then? Because in fact there *was* no conclusion. How *did* it end? With a door slammed shut or one firmly closed? And either way, what *then*? Moving towards the conclusion was easy. But the conclusion itself ...

Julia looked at her watch, grabbed a shopping bag, took her coat from the back of the kitchen door, and with a glance up at receding storm clouds, ran out of the house, slamming the door behind her. As if practising, she thought.

And as if on cue, her neighbour straightened up from behind her hedge, shears in hand. 'Morning, Julia,' Muriel said, ready for talk. And pointing to the shopping bag, 'When is Professor Gibbs – your husband – due home? Today?'

'Yes, today,' Julia said, walking purposefully down the wet path.

'I expect he'll need feeding up,' Muriel called after her, words presumably intended to excuse Julia's un-neighbourly behaviour.

As she stood at the bus stop, it occurred to Julia that Muriel might think of America as a place where people made do with fizzy drinks and beefburgers. She would tell Martin that, make him laugh. And then she remembered why that was the last thing she wanted to do.

**

He contacted her from the train, as promised. 'We've just left Kettering. On the homeward stretch.'

'Right,' she said, her throat so tight she could barely force the word out. She sat for some moments looking at the phone, wondering for one wild moment whether she shouldn't call him back and tell him she wouldn't be at home when he arrived. Or should she tell him not to return at all? You don't belong here, not any longer, not after what you've done. No, impossible. Ridiculous.

What am I to do?

In an agony of indecision she jumped up, went to stand at the kitchen window, staring out at the lawn, trying to regulate her breathing, to concentrate on the tense-wired activity of a robin flirting its wings among the still-green leaves of an acacia bush. Beads of rain-water flecked the paving slabs of the patio beyond the window, the patio Martin himself had laid soon after they moved into this house with the infant Polly more than twenty years ago, and some of the slabs were now cracked and tufts of grass grew between them, the grass that springs eternal, emblem of survival, of endurance.

Abruptly she turned away, left the kitchen, went into the room that served as her study, stared around, saw the desk piled with essays waiting to be read and marked, shuddered, left, crossed the hall and opened the door to the front room. Should she have bought flowers to put in the hearth? Chrysanthemums? The odour of chrysanthemums. The odour of death. She crossed the room, threw open a window, she must get rid of the faint smell, the smell of a room that, one night apart, has not been used, not been lived in for over a month.

She closed the door, ran on tiptoe upstairs as if she was afraid of waking someone, went into her – their – bedroom, checked that the bed was made – it was, that her clothes were hung – they were, shoes arranged under the chair that stood in the window embrasure – yes, all present and correct, left then and crossed the landing to stand in the bathroom, ran her hand along the rack of towels, checked that the lid of the toothpaste was properly secured, took the lavatory brush from its plastic holder, swirled it round the pan, closed the pan lid, and, standing at the basin, having used a tissue to wipe round the plug, washed and dried her hands, glanced at herself in the mirror and deliberately failed to meet the reflection of her eye, walked as slowly as she could downstairs, re-entered the kitchen, went to the sink, picked up a sponge and drew it vigorously over the draining-board, put it back in the soap dish, went across to the stove, lifted the kettle, shook it, took the kettle to the sink, ran water and filled the kettle, returned the kettle to the stove

... and heard and tried not to hear the key in the front door and stood at the sink, unable to breathe, back turned to the kitchen door as she heard the front door close, heard feet on the hall floor, heard the thump of what must be luggage dropped on the carpet, heard feet coming closer, the kitchen door open and

'Hello,' he said, 'Julia',

and then, as she turned to him,

'What's the matter? You look as if you've seen a ghost,' her husband said.

176

***

It was mid-evening when Martin reappeared. In the intervening hours, between persuading him that whatever was upsetting her could wait, and that he must be in need of sleep, after which they could talk, persuasion he had, reluctantly at first resisted, then more readily agreed to, Julia had tried in various ways not to think of what would happen when, finally, they sat facing each other. But after trying and failing to read a new, prize-winning book of poetry she'd bought earlier in the week, whole pages of which slid by before she was prepared to admit that the lines of print carried no meaning for her, and having then gone into her room and forced herself to read and enter marginal comments on student essays as routine as, with a few exceptions, the essays themselves, she knew what she wanted to do.

She reached for her journal.

Saturday, early evening. Martin is upstairs asleep. An hour ago I went up and peered in on him. He was lying across the bed, fully clothed, and I stood there for several minutes, looking down at his immobile body. He was sound asleep, and for one wild, terrible moment I thought how easy it would be to run downstairs, grab a sharp knife and tiptoe back up, then kneel across the bed and cut his throat. I did kneel on the bed but only to peer closely at where he lay, stubble peppering his cheeks and chin brown from Californian sun, browner than when he left, lips slightly apart, so that I could see the chipped front tooth he acquired, he told me, when as a teenager he fell off his bike while swerving to overtake a milk-float and ended up in the road, the bike on top of him, the milkman swearing at him for being a bloody fool. I told him that a good dentist could easily fix the tooth, but he wouldn't hear of it. A badge of dishonour, he called it, a visible reminder not to act the fool.

But I was glad that it didn't prevent him from those sudden outbursts of impulsive behaviour that drew me to him in the first place. I remember when he first appeared in the room I shared with another English student, and who was away for the weekend – I never found out how he knew. He had an old sheet wrapped round him, broomstick in hand and a plastic bucket on his head, claiming to be a medieval knight looking to rescue a damsel in distress. I asked him how he could know I might be in distress, and he said because he himself was in distress. And that was when he told me he couldn't bear seeing me with his supposed friend and that he was here to place me on his palfry and take me to his castle. What castle? I asked, and he said he was working on

177

it. Then he picked up the book I'd been reading – Dante – said that the best line in the whole of the *Inferno* was 'We read no more that day', and within minutes, so it seemed, we were in bed. And later, when I told him how impressed I was that he had read Dante, he admitted that the line he quoted was the only one he knew, and that he'd come across it in a book of quotations. 'I don't even know where it belongs,' he said. I told him it was from the story of Paolo and Francesca, condemned to the second circle of hell for adulterous love. 'If I could be with you,' he said, 'I could easily endure the tenth circle.' There isn't a tenth circle, I told him, and besides, we're not adulterers.

And some years later, not long after Polly had been born, for his birthday that year I gave him a card which carried a Botticelli illustration of the Paradiso, and wrote in it, 'Look closely and you'll see us in the tenth circle.' Sentimental, yes, but it was how I felt, and when –

She paused in her writing. There was movement above, the opening and closing of the bathroom door, the rush of water, rumble of pipes as the shower was activated. Julia capped her pen, closed the journal and returned it to the drawer from where she'd taken it, locked the drawer, pushed the key into her jeans pocket and stood.

She was once more in the kitchen, but this time facing him as he entered, hair damp, dressed in an old sweater and tracksuit bottoms, his bare feet, she noticed, as tanned as his face and neck.

Crossing to the table, he pulled out a chair and sat, legs crossed, elbow resting on the table, newly-shaved chin propped on his closed hand, looking enquiringly at her. 'Well?' he said.

She nerved herself to look steadily at him, but said nothing.

He tried again. 'Are you going to tell me what this is all about?'

Still she said nothing.

He sighed, baffled, frustrated, and, as he spoke, increasingly angry. 'I've been away for a month, four weeks during which you've made no attempt to contact me and whenever I've tried to contact *you* I've been cut off with barely a word. Something is up. What? Polly hasn't a clue what's got into you.' He paused, looked at her intently. 'Have you taken a lover?'

'Would you like a drink?'

'A drink?' His frown became a smile, wry, resigned. 'Why? To soften the blow?' Then, 'I'd like a glass of white wine if we have any.'

She stood, crossed to the fridge, took a bottle from it, brought it to him, pointed to the wine glass she'd already placed on the table, and said, 'Help yourself.' And when he gestured to enquire about her joining him, she shook her head. 'I'm not drinking at the moment,' she told him.

He uncorked the bottle, poured himself a full glass, swallowed a mouthful, said, 'OK. I'm ready. Now can we *please* begin?'

For answer, she took the note from her jeans pocket, smoothed it open as she laid it before him. But she said nothing, merely watched for his reaction.

He picked the note up, frowning slightly, read it, and laid it down beside his wine glass. He looked from note to her and back again. 'Where on earth did this come from?' he asked. His voice gave nothing away. Or, no, she thought, he sounded genuinely puzzled. He was acting, he *must* be acting.

'It was in your dictionary.'

His look was – was what? Sceptical? Disbelieving?

'I was looking up the meaning of a word – "serried" if you must know – and the note fell out.'

He shook his head, grimaced as if in pain, or was it irritation. 'And when was this?'

'Soon after you'd left. Though I don't see that *when* I found it is relevant. It's *what* I found that counts. What the note *says*.'

She stood above him, but her head was turned away.

Martin picked up the note, held it stretched between his hands. 'Almost from the time I got to America I thought something was odd – wrong.'

'And you passed your suspicions on to your friend Giles.'

'How do you know that? Has Giles contacted you?'

'No.' Julia sat once more, facing her husband. 'Trudy told me, after Giles returned from the all-conquering lectures you arranged for him to give. He dropped in on her and James.'

Martin put the note back down on the table.

'Trudy and I have become good friends,' Julia said. 'She and James are planning to marry soon. A good idea, I think, marrying later rather than earlier. Sow your wild oats first.' Her hands, legs, her whole body was

179

shaking. 'Sandra,' she said, and again, though this time she was yelling the name, '*Sandra!* What did you *do*, Martin? What have you *done*?'

'I tried to help,' he said.

'*Help*?' She was incredulous with anger. 'You make a student pregnant and then try to palm her off on an old friend. "Here, Giles, see if you can sort this mess out."' Though even as she was speaking the words they sounded absurd, so that his 'Oh, for Christ's sake don't be ridiculous' came more as confirmation than rebuke. But now she was standing again, her legs steadier, arms propped on the table as she stared into her husband's upturned face.

He met her gaze full on. 'The note you found says no more than that Sandra Hutchinson wanted my help with a problem I thought small enough, but which unfortunately was too much for her.'

'That you'd got her pregnant.'

'You know,' he said, 'I doubt when she killed herself she even knew she was pregnant. She certainly didn't kill herself because of that.'

'I don't believe you,' Julia said.

He got to his feet and for a moment she wondered whether he was going to hit her. But he brushed past her, went to the sink and, using his empty wine glass, filled it with tap water.

He was playing for time, she thought.

Coming back to the table and leaning against his chair, he said, pointing at the note, 'Like many another student in her position, the poor girl had convinced herself she was going to make a mess of her final exams. "I can't go on." Meaning "What's the point of taking any more papers?"'

They were standing very close to each other, staring into each other's eyes. 'And now explain "Tomorrow will be too late",' Julia said.

'What do *you* think it means?' he asked her.

'Isn't it obvious? That unless you went to her that night she'd kill herself.'

Martin looked at her, then away, then back again. 'Yes,' he said, slowly. He sighed, looked away. 'I'm afraid you're right,' he said.

26

SATURDAY EVENING, LATE. MARTIN HAS GONE back to bed and I'm here, in my study, trying to make sense of what he said, trying to decide how much I believe of what he told me. All? Some? Nothing? He swears that he never laid a finger on the girl, never even realised how emotionally dependent she was on him. He didn't deny that she sought him out for advice on rather more occasions than seemed necessary, persisting even when he made it clear – so he says – that she couldn't expect him to go beyond the call of duty, couldn't risk being accused of favouritism by the other students in her year; but he thought her neediness, while vexatious, was prompted by an almost pathological anxiety to do well in her exams. By chance he'd been away from the university the day she put the note in his pigeon-hole, because although, as she'd have known, he was usually committed that day to first-year lectures and tutorials, he was in fact taking students to look round an Elizabethan house in Derbyshire. So he didn't find the note until the following mid-morning, by which time Sandra Hutchinson's body had already been discovered. He insists that he had no idea she was in such a desperate state – which *may* have been partly caused by her realisation that she was pregnant but was more probably because she feared she was making a balls-up of her exams, in which case she wouldn't qualify for a research studentship. To be honest, he said, he didn't think she was up to research, but he was pretty sure that for her it mattered supremely, not so much for itself but in order to prove her worth to the other students, among whom he suspected she wasn't popular. And, knowing of her determination to go on to research, he'd contacted Giles to ask him to take the girl on. She knew about this, of course, because he'd told her. He had also shown her Giles's reply, in which his friend had said that quite by chance he did have a vacancy for a research student, that anyone recommended by Martin was, he was sure, eminently suitable for work in his, Giles's, department, and that subject to a satisfactory interview he would be happy to personally supervise Miss Hutchinson's work. At the time, Martin said, he thought she was comforted by the evidence of his wanting to help her, though after her death he was forced to wonder whether she'd seen it as a form of rejection.

She wasn't good enough for the great Martin Gibbs, I said.

If he heard my words, he didn't show it. Instead, and pursuing his own line of thought, he said, we don't even know she meant to kill herself. She might very well have been hoping that she would be discovered in time.

It was possible. I remembered that Trudy had suggested as much. But supposing, just supposing, Sandra's death was an accident, I said, it still didn't explain why Martin was so keen to pass Sandra onto Giles. I thought I'd made that plain, Martin said, with a show of irritation. Surely you can understand? I was simply trying to do what I thought best. I knew Giles was anxious to boost his department's research rating and that a student recommended by Professor Gibbs to work with him would be sure to gain him brownie points. And if that sounds vainglorious, sorry, but there it is.

He sat, his gaze challenging me to accept his words. But after a minute he admitted that with hindsight he was, he realised, partly prompted by an uneasy sense that Sandra Hutchinson was becoming a bit too close to him for comfort, and that at some level he didn't want to think that this may have prompted him to recommend her to Giles.

And her pregnancy?

Martin was upset about this, *very* upset. Had I ever seen Sandra he asked? Of course, I hadn't, I said. Well, Martin said, she was a bit of a mess. Wore clothes that seemed to come from the nearest reject pile, never seemed to wash her hair, was a loner. As far as he could tell, she had few if any friends, lived, he thought, in digs somewhere on her own, and in class made a point of sitting apart from other students in her tutorial group, getting her rejection in first, you could say. The revelation that she was pregnant came as a total surprise to him as, he was pretty sure, it must have come to anyone who knew her. Perhaps, out of sheer desperation, she'd dragged some male student into bed and this was the result. It was unutterably sad. It also left him feeling guilty. Because if, as he sometimes found himself thinking, it had followed from her being shown Giles's letter, then Sandra quite possibly decided that he, Martin, was making plain that he wanted rid of her.

When Martin looked across at me, I could see that he was genuinely upset. He'd been carrying her note around with him, intending to destroy it, he said, but when he heard the coroner's full report, he felt that in some way he owed it her to keep something of hers, the thought of her disappearing without trace was so *awful*. And by the way, he added, she was right to fear the worst about her exams. The papers she had completed before her death were mediocre at best. Putting her note to him in among the dictionary *S*s was a form of commemoration, a tiny relic of a sad, scarcely visible life, not something he could give her parents, let alone show to the police, but a way of keeping *something* to prove she had actually existed. I had no reason to feel guilty, he said, but I did feel a measure of – well of anguish over her lonely death, her wasted life.

So he hadn't invited Giles over to San Francisco to repay a favour? What favour? Martin asked crossly. Then, Oh, for god's sake, Julia. You mean for offering to take that poor girl off my hands all those years ago? I've already explained about that. I was simply doing an old friend a favour.

Again, he was staring at me, unblinking, unchallengeable, and I have to admit that if all the rest he'd told me was true then so was his insistence that he got Giles the invitation to lecture out of kindness to an old friend. And also, he said with a flash of professional pride, 'because I could.'

And Orlando? Why was he there?

According to Martin, Giles took his son with him because Orlando was at a loose end, though Martin suspects that it was also an opportunity for father and son to 'bond', try to repair their relationship and, Giles being Giles, for father to show son that he was an intellectual heavyweight, whose name carried well beyond the confines of English academia.

I wanted, oh, how I wanted, to ask him whether he had questioned Orlando about our meeting in Brighton, but I couldn't bring myself to do it, and Martin himself didn't bring the matter up. But it's quite possible that Orlando said something which inadvertently aroused Martin's suspicions about why I was there. And my subsequent near-silence must have sharpened his sense, apprehension, that the distance between us wasn't merely geographical. Something had happened to establish radio silence between us. As a result, Martin even thought I had begun an affair.

Do I believe it all? All that Martin has told me, all that I surmise?

Julia stopped writing. Looking out of the kitchen window into the blackness of the October night, she thought, of course it would be perfectly possible to construct an entirely different story to account for that note. And once more, she found herself recalling the words she had first read on the train to Brighton a month earlier: 'Though reason proves/Love deceives at every turn ... ' What came next? Words she couldn't for the moment bring to mind although she knew how the sentence finished. 'Still our actions are compelled by it. It's all we own.'

In the morning she would show the journal she had been keeping to

Martin. Let him make of it what he would. He would perhaps like to know about Tony Rayburn. He *needed* to know, know that Tony owed the research scholarship that began his own career, in part, at least, to Sandra Hutchinson's death. And Martin also needed to know that his own wife had come near to using Tony as a means of – ah, now she remembered the words – handing back the ring, breaking every vow. But would he believe what she had written? Would he understand, even?

Sandra's note, she noticed, was still lying on the table where Martin left it when he went up to bed. Should she tear it up, throw it away? But no, it wasn't hers to destroy. She looked at it one last time, those words of a desperately unhappy young woman scrawled on a scrap of paper and left to be found by the man who wasn't her lover. Julia reached for the note, folded it over, then got to her feet.

Standing at the sink, rinsing Martin's used wine glass, she remembered that Polly would be phoning in the morning, eager to speak to her father. Polly, who would want to tell him about herself and Al, who, in reply to a dutiful question, would expect to be told that he was looking forward to seeing her just as soon as she and Al could tear themselves away from London and spend a night in the provincial backwater where her parents mouldered their time away. That gently mocking tone he so often used when talking to his daughter, a way of speaking his love.

Before leaving the kitchen Julia went to straighten her chair and as she did so a thought flashed through her. Sandra had hanged herself by kicking away the chair she stood on. That had been in her room, hadn't it? And Sandra had expected – hoped – Martin would find her before she died. *So Martin must have known where she lived.* And yet he'd said that he 'thought' she lived alone in digs, had suggested to Julia – no, had wanted her to believe – that he had no idea of Sandra's domestic arrangements.

How did he know? *Why?*

Julia snapped off the kitchen light and marched upstairs. If Martin was asleep she would wake him. This couldn't wait. He must be made to answer. And as she came to that decision, another thought arrived.

184

He'd said, hadn't he, that the girl, that Sandra, wasn't up to research. And yet years earlier, at the time she was his student, he'd sung the girl's praises, called her outstanding, or words to that effect. *Then* she'd been the very model of an aspiring undergraduate, *now* she'd apparently been nothing of the sort. She'd killed herself because she knew she wasn't good enough. A likely story.

She went into their bedroom. Martin was awake, the bedside light illuminating his face as he watched her approach.

'Now,' she said, standing beside the bed, and staring down at him, 'I want to hear the story about Sandra Hutchinson all over again. And this time I want the truth.'

VI

27

'THIS,' GILES SAID, WAVING HIS FORK over a metal dish as if to cense it, 'is as good as ever.' He swallowed a last piece of grilled octopus and looked benignly round the table. 'And so, I venture to suggest, is all that we have eaten.' He looked at the dishes, most of them emptied now of food. 'Moussaka, spanakopita, sagonaki ... Some things never change.'

Julia, facing the sea, was smiling as she watched a man of mountainous proportions sprawled on the sand while two small children played about him. Then the inevitable happened. One of the children ran with a toy bucket down to the shore line, dipped the bucket into the water, returned extravagantly on tiptoe, and tipped the bucket's contents over her father's vast belly. Squeals of delight and terror as he roared, sat up, grabbed the little girl's ankle, dandled her above his open mouth, pretending to take bites out of her leg.

Martin, sitting opposite, turned to follow the direction of her gaze. Having wriggled free of her father's clasp, the little girl was running up the beach towards a woman in a floral pink bikini who was lying face down on a recliner. 'They were certainly here last year,' he said, speaking to the table at large as he turned back to his food.

'Like us,' James said.

'You see.' Giles raised his arms as though inviting applause. 'Some things never change.'

'And others do,' Julia said. She smiled at Trudy sitting between James and Martin. 'And by the way, that isn't the same family. Last year's had three children, besides which, these two little kids are at least a couple of years younger.'

'Well,' Tessa said to Giles, 'that rather puts you in your place.' She lay back in her chair, tilting her face briefly into the sun, then, straightening up, once more came back under the table-umbrella's shade. Her skin gleamed like ivory against her black halter-neck dress, her handsome, lean features unprepared for sun. As always, she would be with them for a few days only, a tangential member of their group. Having arrived on the island the previous evening, she was only now able to congratulate Trudy on her pregnancy.

'When is it due?' she asked, her voice a measured drawl, polite rather than interested.

For answer, Trudy stood, her saffron-coloured smock bulging slightly, her face glowing with delight, as she said, 'Guess.'

She was inviting them all, although Julia – and of course James – knew the answer.

Tassos came across the sand from the taverna's kitchen bearing a tray on which were plates of baklava and an alp of yoghurt studded with pistachio nuts and darkened by rivulets of honey. Spoon handles like metal quills stuck out from its flanks. In the act of positioning the plates on their table, he paused, looked at Trudy, and, as he gestured to her stomach, announced, 'Welcome to the world, my young friend. Next year you will eat the good food of Tassos's Taverna.'

'I'll drink to that,' James said.

He got to his feet and motioned the others to rise. And, in their shorts and singlets, raising glasses of retsina, beer, and water, they toasted Trudy's unborn child.

* * *

The following morning Julia and Trudy agreed to meet for coffee while the men were at a bar. They had invited Tessa to join them but she said no, if they didn't mind, she wanted to trawl the shops in a search for gifts to take back for Orlando and his bride-to-be. Unlike the no-tears-no-fuss wedding of Trudy and James, attended by very few, though the meal

190

afterwards at a Thai restaurant was fun, Giles had taken pains when they'd first met up again on the island to explain that his son's marriage was to be what he called 'an unavoidably rather grand affair.'

Martin and James exchanged smiles at the tone of would-be rueful regret. The bride, so Giles implied, came from a well-known, or was it old, family.

'Do you think we'll be invited?' Trudy asked Julia, as they sat over their coffees, looking out across the water past the usual clutter of small fishing boats and expensive yachts to where the nearby islet – its name derived from Fish-Hook – glimmered under the flawless summer sky.

'Oh, yes,' Julia said. 'He'll want to show us all off.'

'I don't see what *we've* got to offer,' Trudy said.

'Not you and me,' Julia said. 'But James is a TV Executive ... '

'No, he isn't,' Trudy said.

'He will be when Giles introduces him to the guests. And Martin will be a world-beating Historian.'

Trudy laughed. 'And here was I thinking Orlando was a natural born rebel, sworn off bourgeois life-style. Who *is* he marrying, do you know?'

'No idea. Martin says it's probably some perfectly ordinary girl who's going to be transformed by a wave of Giles's wand into a grand duchess.'

Turning away from her friend and looking along the promenade where fishermen sat cross-legged to mend their nets, Trudy said, 'How have you and Martin been getting on?'

Julia waited for several motor-bikes to roar past before she said, 'OK.' Then, drinking the last of her coffee, she amended this to, 'Well enough.'

She and Trudy had last talked not long before both couples were due to fly to Athens, but that had been brief, purposeful. Times of arrival, information about ferry sailings. Most of their recent conversations had been by phone, including Trudy's announcement of her pregnancy, though before then Julia, whenever she paid a weekend visit to London to stay with Polly, invariably found time to spend an hour or two with her friend. Having discovered a shared pleasure in looking at pictures, they would occasionally meet at galleries; or they window-shopped; or they strolled through parks – Greenwich, with its hill-top panoramic views was a particular favourite especially as, to reach it, they could take a boat downstream from the Embankment and then return via the Dockland Light Railway, that allowed them to stare out at multi-storey towers walled by opaque glass through which clouds and air seemingly passed without hindrance, and which were intersected by river inlets and basins where unmanned boats rode without purpose at anchor, and they could gaze at what Trudy, in mock tourist-guide voice, called 'future London' taking shape, a city of human effacement, though from time to time the glimpse of an ordinary street below them with people walking along it suggested a momentary time warp in which, for as long as it lasted, they were back in the all-but-forgotten twenty-first century.

Julia delighted in Trudy's inventive wit, her ability to transform whatever she saw into something at once fantastical and entirely plausible, her relish for the oddities and out-of-the-way experiences she didn't so much go looking for as instantly recognise in all that was around her. 'I should have been a bug-hunter with net and khaki shorts,' she remarked on an occasion when Julia was half-laughing, half-marvelling, at her friend's ability to discover in what she called an odds-and-sods shop some piece of junk, improbable uses for which she surmised as she held it up for inspection. 'Either that or an archaeologist. Field work would have suited me, don't you think? Down on hands and knees, looking for clues to ancient civilization.'

'Where sifted and searched in vain, the indiscoverable secret sleeps.'

Trudy cocked an eyebrow. 'You're quoting, I hope.'

'Cowper,' Julia said, 'spelt with a w.'

'Awesome,' Trudy said. 'Spelt without the B.' She was fingering a thin twist of metal, about four inches long. 'Now what do you reckon is this?' And when Julia shook her head, Trudy, leaning in close said, 'An instrument for removing beetles from a nobleman's peruke. No? Well, then perhaps a lady-in-waiting's back-scratcher.'

'Waiting for what?'

'I wouldn't dream of telling you,' Trudy said, twirling the object in her long, elegant fingers. 'Oh, I know. It's a weasel spit. Does them to a turn, as the saying is. OK. Your guess.'

'I give up,' Julia said, though as they continued their trawl she did identify a two-inch high china-clay penguin as a pie-crust holder.

***

One weekend, when Martin was at a three-day conference in Dublin – from where he contacted Julia each morning as though to confirm his whereabouts – Trudy came for an overnight visit. On the Saturday morning they left the house early, having over breakfast decided on a river-bank walk. Muriel was already out in her garden, shears in hand, inspecting her shaven privet, and having been introduced to Trudy she gazed speculatively at Julia's guest before asking after Professor Gibbs. As always, she uttered the title – 'Professor' – with a degree of reverential formality. Martin was away for a few days, she was told, at one of his conferences. Muriel nodded. 'It's good to have a man about the house,' she said, then frowning at what was presumably an extrusive leaf, ducked out of sight and they heard the click of her shears.

'What was that about?' Trudy asked, as, arm-in-arm, the two friends walked to the bus stop.

'Muriel's a professional widow,' Julia said, and then, 'No, I shouldn't have said that. She's lonely.'

'Yes,' Trudy said, 'I can see that.'

'See loneliness?'

They crossed the road and gained the bus-stop before Trudy answered.

'My mother was like that, after my Dad left her. She'd mope at home, and when I told her to get out more she'd put on her overcoat and go and stand on the front lawn, pretending to be busy with gardening duties and hoping that someone passing by would stop for a chat.'

'Was Muriel wearing an overcoat?' Julia asked, abashed.

'She was,' Trudy said, and once they were settled on the bus, Julia had time to think of the occasions she had passed in and out of her own house scarcely noticing the woman next door, offering no more than a nod of the head or, at best, a few polite meaningless words. But then, she thought, I too have been lonely, and immediately rebuked herself. No, not *that* lonely. I have my work, I have my beloved daughter, I have friends, including the one sitting beside me. Correction, *especially* the one sitting beside me. The rest are acquaintances rather than friends.

And it came to her that before Trudy she had done perfectly well, so she had always thought, without close friends. After all, she had Martin.

She turned to Trudy, who was staring out of the window as the bus ran along beside the river with its string of moored narrow boats and river craft making their way downstream. She's much more observant than I am, Julia thought. For a moment she wondered whether to justify what must seem her indifference to Muriel by telling Trudy about the widow's implied disapproval of Al, but at once knew that this would be understood as an excuse for the inexcusable. I owe Muriel an apology, she thought. I must learn to be a better neighbour.

Striding along the tow-path in blustery sunshine, they were hailed from a passing motor boat. 'Two fair lasses do I espy. Hello, darlings, out for a good time?'

As the AUNTIE AGNES puttered close in to the bank, Julia said to Trudy, her spirits unaccountably lifted, 'Oh, god. It's two nautical desperadoes.'

Introductions were made, Ronnie and Graham invited the two aboard, and a boat trip up-river and then down ended with the four of them eating at the pub Ronnie insisted, as always, on calling the Angler's Remains.

Afterward, when they had been deposited on the river bank near to a bus stop, Trudy said, 'Was that pre-arranged?'

Julia shook her head. 'No, I promise. You didn't mind, did you?'

'I loved it,' Trudy said, squeezing Julia's arm, and her candid, exuberant pleasure made it easier for Julia later in the day to tell her friend more than she had hitherto done of what had happened on the evening she referred to as Black Friday, the evening of her accident and all that followed. 'Not that anything much came of it,' she said.

'"It" being this Dr Rayburn, I assume?' Trudy looked enquiringly at Julia.

Should I tell her? Julia wondered. But no. Her single night with Tony, which had happened early in the New Year when Martin was in London for the night, and she and Tony had gone on from the conviviality of the

Royal Oak to a meal in town and then a taxi home, had been one less of passion than of modest satisfaction, from which they had parted as friends but with no suggestion on either side that their intimacy might be renewed.

'Tony is someone I'm very fond of and I'm sorry he'll be leaving,' she said. 'But he's been offered an academic post in America and he's without ties so understandably he'll be off as soon as his college year comes to an end.'

'And no regrets?' Trudy said, the words uttered in such a way as to imply a question.

'None,' Julia said, deliberately misunderstanding. 'He's excited at the chance he's been given, and I'm delighted for him. He deserves it.'

But, to her own surprise, and then relief, she felt less reticent in talking to her about Martin. Trudy already knew about the argument that had inevitably followed Julia's accusation that Martin had deceived her, that he was a liar. It was an accusation he always denied. 'You said you didn't know where she lived, but you did, you did.'

No matter how often she threw the words at him, his reply was the same. 'I didn't.'

How could he expect her to believe that? she wanted to know. His own wife. Did he take her for a fool? *Martin I can't go on. Tomorrow will be too late.* 'She was asking you to go to her. She didn't write down her address. She didn't have to. You knew it, knew where to find her. Why lie?'

'I'm not lying,' he said, the more wearily the more she yelled at him. And once, but once only, as if there was no point in arguing with someone determined not to believe him, he said with a kind of flat finality, 'All I can think is that in her distress, her confusion, Sandra assumed I'd know how to find her.'

'And you expect me to believe that?'

'No,' he said. 'I don't.'

Over the months between Martin's return and the following summer she shared with Trudy something of the distrust, animosity, the deepening desolation between wife and husband, the gathering estrangement that they scarcely bothered to disguise from visitors and acqaintances, although whenever Polly phoned they were able to suggest an amicability which became a matter of shame to Julia and, she suspected, to her husband. Such practised liars they were.

And to all appearances such self-contained, assured units of selfhood. They took it in turns to make dinner which they would eat, sitting opposite each other as they discussed daily matters, though whereas Julia might mention her students – including those she thought unusually gifted and for whom she hoped much as well as others like Grenfell, who had left the college, or been dismissed, it wasn't clear to her which – Martin confined himself to talk of colleagues. Of his students he said nothing.

After they had washed their plates and made and drunk cups of coffee, they went their separate ways, Martin to his study, Julia to hers. And though they sometimes agreed to a cinema outing and, once or twice sat side by side watching a theatrical performance, their conversations never went beyond a certain measured formality. Anyone overhearing them, Julia thought, would take them to be distant or slight acquaintances rather than a couple who knew each other well, let alone husband and wife. By unspoken agreement, Julia occupied their bedroom alone. Martin slept on a couch in his study.

Autumn turned to winter and their domestic arrangement hardened into habit. But then, late one afternoon in early December, Polly phoned to ask if she and Al could come for Christmas. 'Of course,' Julia said, 'Yes,' adding 'I'd love that.'

'And Dad, too, I hope,' Polly was laughing.

'Oh, of course,' Julia said.

When she told Martin that evening, he was first delighted, then, she could see, upset, apprehensive. Neither of them had discussed with their daughter the sundering of her parents' marriage.

'A bit of a problem, that,' he said, as they sat over the remains of the meal he had prepared. It was a fish casserole, the recipe for which he had picked up in San Francisco, and which proved to be a considerable success despite lacking the recommended avocado accompaniment.

'But the Leicester avocado is in short supply at this time of year,' Martin said apologetically.

The flickering approach to wit was, though, snuffed out by Julia's words. 'I don't want Polly to know about us. Not when she and Al will so soon be off to New York.'

No more was said about it, but the night before Polly and Al arrived, Martin returned to the marriage bed, where he and Julia slept back to back.

Did either of the young couple suspect? At odd moments Julia was conscious of Polly looking at her or Martin in a manner that suggested a puzzled awareness of what she might see as an inexplicable, insistent accord between her parents, a show of mutuality which lacked the friendly bickering, those moments which are compensated for by a look, a hand on arm, a touch on the cheek. For of course they couldn't bring themselves to any such shows of affection. Julia's own sense of being separated from Martin by an invisible glass wall was sharpened at these moments, and it was then she would yearn to put an arm round Polly or have Polly do the same to her. Which Polly, being Polly, often did over the three days they were all together, though Julia's joy was lessened by observing that her daughter as frequently embraced her father as she did her mother.

And when, at the end of Boxing Day, after the four of them had been out for what Polly announced to Al was 'The Family Gibbs's Traditional Walk', emphasising the customary nature of their expedition along the towpath, and they had returned to cold meats and mince pie, and Polly and Al were piling presents and bags into their car, Polly hugged both of them, and said with an exuberant grin, 'Next Christmas you'll have to come to us, in New York. Promise now.'

'We promise,' Martin said, and for a moment Julia wondered whether, when she echoed his words, he might go so far as to put an arm round her. But no.

Afterwards, though, Martin didn't go back to the study's couch, and as the New Year turned to spring the cold between Julia and him thawed to a tepid acceptance, and the silent accusations sank from the surface of their lives. From time to time, even, the ache of proximity turned to love making, but it was silent, perfunctory, as though for either of them to speak might be to ruin the fragile assent their actions implied. And indeed a word out of place, a casual, unguarded remark, was liable to set in motion the tremor that brought up, like treacherous rocks exposed by tidal movement, the hidden reef on which their marriage had all but foundered.

At such moments Julia would have to hold herself steady before she could speak. And she would see in Martin's eyes a sudden flare of consternation, though whether he ever *truly* understood she doubted. Perhaps it was that he couldn't bear, or was unable, to acknowledge that he was the shallower of the two, or so she thought. It was a thought which, justified or not, gave her a strange sense of consolation.

***

Early in the summer term, Julia found a message in her pigeon-hole requesting her to attend a meeting with Rudkin and Janine 'at your earliest convenience.'

The meeting took place in Rudkin's office, although the Principal did most of the talking. After the minimum of pleasantries, she said, 'You've probably heard rumours that I have been thinking of taking retirement.'

Puzzled, Julia nodded agreement.

'The college has decided to make an internal promotion to the role of Vice-Principal.' Janine paused. 'The successful candidate is Graham – Graham Richards.'

Another pause, after which Julia said, 'Good for him.'

'You sound surprised?' Janine's smile included an acknowledgement that Graham's promotion wouldn't necessarily be welcome news to all.

But Julia was surprised for a different reason. Graham, she thought, had never made any bones about his dislike of the kind of pompous authority Rudkin embodied. Now, he'd have to work with him. Not only that. Poacher would become gamekeeper. 'Is this common knowledge?' she asked. 'I mean, does the staff as a whole know?' It was certainly news to her.

'They will be told tomorrow.' Rudkin spoke as though it was his reluctant duty to convey to the great unwashed information he'd prefer to keep to himself.

So why am I being favoured? Julia wondered, and as if in answer, Janine said, 'When I depart there will, of course, be a vacancy for my post as English tutor. I'm aware that my administrative responsibilities took me away from teaching rather more than I'd have liked, and that this put pressure on my colleagues, yourself included.' The smile did not suggest that she was in any way apologetic for the little teaching she had done over the past years.

But anyway, who were these colleagues? The Head of English apart, a man Julia rarely if ever saw, there were two other part-timers, young women whose work as evening tutors meant that she had no more than nodding acquaintance with either, although she had heard, from Graham, now she thought of it, that both planned to finish with the college as soon as they could find other work. So when she heard Janine say that many good reports had come to her and the secretary of Julia's teaching skills and of her commitment to the students – here Rudkin did not so much smile assent as grimace – and that, subject to the necessary procedures, the college would like to offer her a full-time, permanent lectureship, she couldn't decide whether to be flattered or forewarned, especially as Janine immediately added that the Head of English would almost certainly himself be taking retirement on the grounds of ill health. Exhausted by all the conferences he has to attend, she thought.

But that evening, when she discussed the offer with Martin, he persuaded her to accept. 'Of course, they'll have to call you to formal interview,' he said, 'They may even have to advertise the post. But they obviously want you. Quite right, too.'

She pretended to ignore the remark. Instead, 'I'm surprised at Graham,' she told him. 'He's always seemed so hostile to the people in suits.'

'The lure of power,' Martin said. 'It gets to people you'd never think would be seduced. Look at Giles. A man less likely ... '

Reaching for the bottle of claret that sat on the table between them, he said, still with a faint smile, 'Perhaps Graham will ask Ronnie to choose a suit for him. That should go down well with this secretary you've mentioned.'

'Rudkin! Speak not of him,' Julia said.

'And don't you go quoting obscure authors,' Martin said. He poured for both of them. 'I propose a toast,' he said. 'To you.'

He raised his glass to her and meeting his eyes, the uncertainty behind his smile, she thought, sadly, he's trying to make amends.

***

Nevertheless, as Julia sat among her friends looking out over the glittering water on the last day of their month together, drowsy under the Aegean sky and the influence of several glasses of retsina, half-listening to Giles's words and conscious from the glances she and Trudy exchanged that she shared her friend's amused tolerance of the man's bland certainties, she was glad that she and Martin were still, as it were, together, still married. Sheltering her gaze behind dark glasses, she studied her husband and, finding his eyes were on her, watchful, thoughtful, she smiled briefly at him, and, not, she hoped out of habit, he smiled back.

Yes, she thought, taking in those who sat round the table before she turned eyes once more on Martin, who was still watching her, conspiratorial now, even, who knew, hopeful, it's as the poet says, though love deceives at every turn, it's all we own.

Acknowledgements

Grateful thanks to all at Greenwich Exchange and especially to Janet Davidson and Patrick Ramsey for their editorial labours. Thanks, too, to Rachel Lucas for reading and commenting on an earlier version of the novel. Many thanks to Emma Lucas for useful information about the ways of Colleges of Further Education.

The poem 'XXX' is by Michael Murphy and can be found in his *Collected Poems*, Shoestring Press, 2009.